The Black Pill

(A Jackson & Dallas Thriller)
By L.J. Sellers

THE BLACK PILL

Cover art by David MacFarlane
Ebook formatting by Barb Elliott

ISBN: 978-1-7345418-1-6
Published in the USA by Spellbinder Press

Cast of Characters:

Wade Jackson: detective/Violent Crimes Unit

Katie Jackson: Jackson's daughter

Kera Kollmorgan: Jackson's girlfriend/nurse

Lara Evans: detective/task force member

Rob Schakowski (Schak): detective/task force member

Michael Quince: detective/task force member

Denise Lammers: Jackson's supervisor/sergeant

Sophie Speranza: newspaper reporter

Jasmine Parker: evidence technician

Joe Berloni: evidence technician

Jamie Dallas: FBI undercover specialist

Bettina Rios: missing woman

Carl Jagger: homicide victim

Sam Turnbull: Carl's brother

Aaron Russo: suspect

Chapter 1

Saturday, September 14, 6:27 a.m.
Bettina Rios pulled on running shoes, grabbed her cell phone from the dresser, and clicked the Strava icon. But she wouldn't start the mileage app yet. First she had to check on her mother. Across the hall, she tapped lightly on the other bedroom door. "Mama? You awake?"

"Si."

Bettina stepped in, braced for the clutter and smell. Her mother loved glass figurines and tacky paintings and had managed to accumulate a substantial collection in the short time they'd been there. The old woman sat in her wheelchair, wearing stained sweatpants and a red sweater with holes in it, her gray hair a mess. She only changed clothes when Bettina helped her shower. Her mother hated the whole undignified process, so they didn't do it often.

"How are you?" Bettina always spoke English to Mama and encouraged her to do the same. The skill might save their lives someday.

"I no sleep." Her weak voice made Bettina's heart hurt. Mama had been so strong, so fearless. But the long journey had taken its toll, and now she couldn't do much of anything.

"Maybe less coffee." Bettina smiled gently, knowing she had wasted her breath. Her mother ate and drank whatever

4

she wanted. That's how she'd ended up in this mess. The stubborn woman was probably diabetic but wouldn't see a doctor or take any help from "strangers." So Bettina did it all. The situation was challenging to work around, so she kept their finances afloat with gig jobs. Her main one was really strange, but paid well.

She kissed Mama's forehead and wheeled her into the kitchen. "Fruit and toast?"

"Just toast. With *mermalada*." A crooked smile eased onto her sun-weathered face. "That counts as fruit."

"Sure." Bettina fixed whatever made her mother happy. Today, that was toast spread thick with strawberry jam. She noticed the fridge was low on cheese and wine, the two things her mother loved most, so she would make a trip to the store later. After handing over the plate, Bettina asked, "What else can I do for you?"

"*Nada*. Later, you can help me write to Ernesto." Bettina's older brother was still in their home country. Mama waved a crippled blue-veined hand. "Go run. I'll be fine."

Feeling guilty as usual, Bettina headed out, locking the door behind her. On the sidewalk, she pressed the Strava record button and the screen changed to a map. She clicked Start and slid the phone into her fanny pack.

Jogging down the quiet, low-rent street, she squinted in the near darkness. Her eyes would adjust soon, and the sun would rise before she finished her run. She didn't care for the darkness, but in the summer months, she liked to get her workout done before the temperature rose and before she showered and dressed for the day. Using the Strava app was rather silly because she didn't vary her route much. But she liked keeping track of her miles and being connected to others who were as obsessed with exercise as she was. All of it helped keep her accountable. If she skipped a day, one of her followers would ping her and want to know why. She did the same for them.

A wave of apprehension rolled over her. Would her ex-boyfriend use the app as a way to get to her? What a mistake he'd been. So emotional and possessive. But she'd been lonely for so long that she'd let her guard down and trusted a *chico sexy* who'd smiled at her in that special way. Bettina shook it off, reassuring herself again that using Strava was fine. Aaron didn't exercise and wasn't tech savvy, so he'd never find her that way. The loneliness of her life was nearly unbearable, and the low-key social network gave her some interaction.

At the corner, she turned left on Lombard and headed toward the river park. From there, she would run north on the bike path to the Owosso bridge, cross over, and run back on the other side of the river. The whole loop, including the five blocks to and from her house, covered four and a half miles. She'd hoped to improve her conditioning over time, but the extra weight on her petite body slowed her down.

She'd been running her whole life, one way or another. As a kid, she'd dashed around the beach with her brother, a never-ending game of chase. Years later, when her breasts developed, she'd run from gang members who wanted to rape her and claim her as their property. After they'd caught her, she and Mama had left the first time. Now she jogged to keep her brain from going *loco*—and to burn off all the cheese and chocolate she loved to eat.

Bettina approached the narrow entrance to the park and tensed, wishing for a little more daylight. Overgrown with trees on both sides, the tucked-away access lane was the only part of the route that made her feel vulnerable. She touched the canister of mace she wore around her neck and picked up her pace. As she rounded the turn, she heard something snap. Bettina jerked her head toward the noise. Nothing but eerie shadows under the overhanging trees. Relieved to see the parking lot ahead, she smiled at her own jitters.

Soft footsteps rustled in the other direction. She spun toward the sound, and a dark figure rushed at her. *No!* In a flash, he grabbed her ponytail and jerked her toward him with stunning force. Bettina opened her mouth to scream, but his hand clamped over it. An acrid scent burned her nose.

Oh god! He was drugging her! She reached for her mace, but dizziness overcame her. A powerful arm squeezed around her shoulders, dragging her into the trees. As her world started to go black, her last thought was, *I'm so sorry, Mama!*

Chapter 2

Tuesday, September 17, 5:45 p.m.
Detective Wade Jackson reached for his service weapon, and a terrifying scream erupted behind him. He spun around, heart pounding. The scream became a wail of agony. He started forward, then remembered the Sig Sauer holstered against his ribs. He pulled the gun, shoved it into a case on the dresser, and slammed the locking lid.

A quick sprint into the hall brought him face-to-face with the problem. Two four-year-old boys had a death grip on a plastic dinosaur toy and neither would let go. The wailing came from Micah, Kera's grandson, who was temperamental. The poor child had been in transition for most of his short life and had lost his mother the previous year.

"I had it first." Benjie, his adopted son, was emphatic, yet calm. He'd not only lost his mother, he'd also witnessed her murder. Yet the tragic event had given him a strange mature serenity. Jackson worried that Benjie was suppressing his anxiety, but counseling hadn't brought it out.

Jackson held out a hand. "Give it to me, please."

Benjie quickly let go, forcing Micah to be the one to hand it over. An act that made his stepbrother sob.

Kera popped out of the bathroom. "What's going on?" Tall and gorgeous, his girlfriend was always a pleasure to his weary eyes.

"Same old stuff." Jackson handed her the toy. "We need two of these."

"We have two!" Kera looked back and forth between the boys. "Where's the other one?"

Micah shrugged, and Benjie looked thoughtful. "Maybe in the toy box."

"Well, go find it. You're not getting this one back until you do." She shooed them off and leaned in to kiss Jackson. "I love it when you're home early and we can be a normal family."

Jackson laughed. "I'm not sure there's anything normal about our scenario, but I'm happy to be here." *Sort of.* Living full-time with Kera and Micah was more challenging than he'd imagined. Having a second young child in the house generated an energy and volume he wasn't prepared for—and the more time the boys spent together, the more they fought. His daughter Katie, almost a legal adult now, had been quiet and easy as a little kid.

Jackson suppressed a sigh, followed Kera to the kitchen, and started chopping the onion she handed him. "How was your day?" he asked.

"Good." She put down the big knife she'd just picked up. "But I think I made a mistake in taking the job at the fertility clinic. It's so boring."

"You mean compared to Planned Parenthood." Jackson grinned. "I knew you would miss the chaos."

She smiled too. "It's more about missing the variety of patients. I never knew who would be waiting in the exam room. All walks of life."

"Yeah, I get that in my job too." Jackson squeezed her arm. "So go back to Planned Parenthood. You know they'll be glad to have you."

"It pays less."

"I know. We'll be fine. You need to enjoy your work."

"Thanks for that."

"Of course."

After dinner, Jackson sat on the living-room floor with the boys, surrounded by a rainbow of toy blocks. They constructed a variety of towers, tearing each one down with gusto before starting another. Next they built a mutant vehicle. He yearned for one of the kids to show an interest in real cars someday. His daughter had helped him restore a '69 GTO, but she'd done it out of obligation rather than real passion, and he'd had to sell it after his divorce. They'd also built a three-wheeled vehicle he still drove sometimes. Now that he and Kera were settled into this big rental home, he was eager to get started on a new project.

When Micah got tired and cranky, Kera read a story to the boys, then Jackson helped them get ready for bed.

"Remember, tomorrow is park day." Benjie hugged him with a tight squeeze. "I love you, Daddy." The words melted his heart every time.

He and Kera changed into pajamas, got into bed to watch a movie, and fell asleep before it ended.

Jackson woke to his phone ringing. Startled and confused, he sat up, glancing at the digital clock: *12:45 a.m.* He snatched his phone from the nightstand. *Sergeant Lammers.* A strange mix of dread and adrenaline surged through him. Plus another emotion he couldn't identify.

"Is it work?" Kera mumbled, sitting up.

He nodded, climbed out of bed, and headed into the hall for privacy. "Hey, Sarge. What have we got?"

"A dead body in the road at the corner of Greenhill and

Highway 126." A pause. "I need you to take it."

"A traffic accident?" He knew better.

"No. The victim is wrapped in plastic, and a woman motorist ran over it."

What? "That's a new one."

"Indeed. That's why I called you. Besides, everyone else is already overworked."

A flash of guilt. "Do we know anything yet?"

"No. The responding patrol officer dragged the body off the road for safety but didn't try to unwrap it."

"Good. I need to see it as is." The scene flashed in his mind. A dark roadside clusterfuck—right on the edge of the city limits. "But the location is inside the boundary?"

"We're assuming so."

"Do I get a team?" The Violent Crimes Unit was overwhelmed, as always, but this time it was mostly his fault for taking medical leave for the first half of the month.

"I'll send Evans out, and we'll see what develops."

"I'm on my way." Jackson stepped back into the bedroom.

Kera was on her feet now. "A new homicide?"

"An odd one. I'll tell you what I can when I know more."

"I'll make you coffee while you get dressed."

"Thank you!" She was so good to him. He pulled on the same clothes he'd been wearing earlier and retrieved his weapon from the fingerprint safe. He hated leaving the house in the middle of the night, but at least now he didn't have to wake up his kids and take them to a sitter when it happened. He'd only had a small window of time between when his daughter was old enough to be left alone and when Benjie came into his life.

Jackson stopped, suddenly worried. *Where was Katie?* Had she come home while he was asleep? No, he would have woken at the sound. Another curfew violation. Her new boyfriend obviously didn't respect house rules.

In the kitchen, while Jackson located his travel mug, Kera said, "I used the Keurig because it's faster, but don't worry, the brew is strong."

He transferred the coffee, then hugged her. "Will you try to track down Katie? I don't have the time or focus right now."

"I'll text her."

"Thanks." Jackson tried not to look, or feel, upset. "I'll probably be back around four in the morning for a couple hours of sleep."

"Are you sure you're ready for this? Your surgery was less than a month ago."

"I'm fine. Yes, the incision still hurts, but it's different. A healing pain and fading fast." The abdominal fibrosis would likely grow back again, but he refused to worry about it until it happened. "We're too short-handed for me to sit out any longer."

"And you love your work." Kera smiled.

"It's who I am." Jackson kissed her and headed out.

In the driveway, he noticed Katie's car parked on the street in front of the house. That meant her boyfriend was with her and that Ethan would likely borrow the Honda and drive it home. Jackson hated both thoughts. He jogged over, wincing at the sight of them making out in the backseat. Would he ever get used to the idea that his daughter was a sexual person?

He slapped the roof hard. "Wrap it up. Katie has a curfew!" If not for his new case, he would have hung around and made them uncomfortable.

But he was already running late. Jackson hurried to his city-issued sedan. Behind the wheel, he gunned the engine for effect as he backed out of the driveway, then stopped parallel with the other vehicle. Katie glared and rolled her eyes. Jackson pointed at the house, unsmiling. He'd accepted long ago that he had no real control over his daughter, but he maintained the right to have rules if she wanted to live in his house. Or his rental anyway. He and Kera had signed a six-month lease on this place, giving them time to look for a house to purchase. But he wasn't in any rush, and he and his brother still owned the house they'd grown up in.

As Jackson drove off, he pushed the family stuff out of his head. He had a murder victim waiting and justice to pursue.

Chapter 3

Jackson cruised through the downtown area, where barhopping college students and homeless people still roamed the sidewalks. He had a flash of sympathy for his patrol colleagues who had to deal with both—but not for much longer. When the weather turned and winter set in, the streets would be a dead zone at this hour. In the meantime, most officers never had to look at dead bodies, so there were some benefits to wearing a uniform.

As he drove west, he was reminded of other homicides he'd been assigned. One in particular had been a young woman brutally beaten and left in her own car, not far from where he was now headed. *Please don't let this death be female!* The mindless plea made him shake his head. It was too late for God, or the universe, or whatever, to intervene.

Speeding along in the dark, with the main road nearly to himself, kept his pulse at an elevated rate. He was used to the adrenaline rush of having a new investigation. Especially right now. For the past few months—before and after his surgery—he'd been helping the DA build a court case against the last murder perp he'd arrested, work that was tedious and unsatisfying. The chase was so much more interesting. Jackson forced himself to acknowledge the other emotion playing under the surface. *Relief.* The case would take him out of the house in the evenings and away from the intense domesticity. The realization made him feel guilty . . . but human. Most people lived every day in the struggle between seeking stimulation and craving tranquility.

After he passed the big-box stores at the edge of town, the landscape grew dark. Flashing red-and-blue lights in the distance soon signaled the location a mile up the road. A few minutes later, the neon glow of a gas station came into view. He expected the scene at the intersection to be chaos. But if the body was wrapped in plastic, the victim had likely been killed elsewhere. Would he be able to find the primary crime scene? The car in front slowed, so he did too. Had officers blocked the road? As a main artery between Eugene and the coast, they couldn't hold traffic for too long. Even at this hour.

No vehicles were coming from the other direction, so Jackson eased around the two slow-moving cars ahead. A moment later, an officer in the middle of the road signaled for him to stop, then ran up to the car. Jackson rolled down his window, noting that the patrol cop was young and male and not someone he knew.

"Detective Jackson, EPD. I've been assigned this case."

"Yes, sir. You can park at the gas station. The body is on the opposite corner."

"Are you letting any traffic through?"

"Yes, but we're stopping everyone and taking names and plate numbers."

"Good." Jackson was skeptical that the process would produce anything helpful, but it made sense to try. He eased forward and pulled into the paved parking area filled with first responders: three dark-blue SUV patrol units, a sedan with no markings, and an ambulance. Paramedics stood beside the rig, their services apparently not needed.

As Jackson climbed out, Detective Lara Evans hurried over from the convenience store. The sight of her jolted him with emotions—love, longing, regret. He'd been her mentor, then they'd become dear friends . . . and eventually they'd had a few tender moments. But Kera and the boys needed him, so he shut down those feelings and focused on his respect for Evans. Her petite body and sweet face belied a physical strength that could be intimidating. She'd passed the SWAT physical to become the only woman on the team, and she'd quickly become an excellent detective.

She flashed him a smile. "Hey, Jackson. Good to have you back out in the field."

"Thanks." He nodded. "What do you know? How freaky is this one?"

"Very. The body is across the street." She pointed at an angle toward an empty corner lot. "It's still wrapped, of course. My best guess is that it fell out of a vehicle, possibly as the driver rounded the corner."

"You think the corpse rolled out of the back of a truck?"

"Exactly. The plastic has scuff marks." She paused. "And tire marks. Let's walk over."

They started across the dark intersection, the only real light coming from the business behind them and a faint green glow from the traffic signal above. A patrol SUV in the empty lot aimed its headlights toward the road, and another vehicle sat off to the side. Evans pointed at the small car. "That's the driver who ran over the body, then called it in. Marlie Canasta. The poor woman is pretty upset, but I made her wait in case you wanted to talk to her."

Jackson was torn. He wanted to question the witness and let her go, but he had to see the victim first. Evans led him to where three patrol officers stood near the road. A narrow drainage ditch ran alongside the asphalt, but the fall rain hadn't started yet so it was filled with dry grass. On the ground lay a six-foot roll of black plastic secured with bungee cords. The body shape was obvious and, based on the size, most likely male.

The officers turned. John Durham, who'd taken his crime scene class long ago, spoke up. "Detective Jackson. What's the protocol?"

"Hell if I know." His impulse was to cut open the plastic. "Who was first on the scene?"

"I was, sir," Durham said. "I dragged the victim off the road." He pointed to a spot about fifty yards from the intersection. "It was right in the middle."

"Where was the driver who ran over the body?"

"Right where she is now." The officer shifted and shook his head. "She says she didn't see it at all. After the thump, she pulled off the road and ran back to see what she'd hit. Then called 911."

"Is she believable?"

"Yes, sir. She's pretty shaken up."

Evans had thought so too. Jackson glanced at the city lights in the distance, wondering when the medical examiner would arrive. Gunderson would want him to wait to touch the body, but time was essential. They had to figure out who the victim was. "Any witnesses?"

Evans cut in. "The driver says she was the only car in the area at the time. I also questioned the employee over at the gas station. He didn't see or hear anything unusual, nor did he serve a customer in a truck prior to the event."

Jackson's phone rang, lighting up in his jacket pocket: *Lammers*. He took the call. "Sergeant."

"Gunderson is running late. But he wants you to leave the

plastic intact and let him deal with it in the morgue."

"I need to ID this victim. A face, a name, something to go on. What if he or she lives right around here? Or was killed nearby? What if the perp is sitting just down the road, confused and scared, and ready to confess?"

A pause.

"It's your call." Lammers clicked off.

Jackson knelt down and took several photos with his cell phone. They wouldn't be worth much without proper light, but he had to document everything as much as he could. A tear in the plastic at the other end caught his eye. Scooting toward it, he realized the section had been cut. He looked at Evans. "You opened it?"

"I needed to see if the victim was still alive." A little defensiveness in her tone. "It would have been irresponsible not to check for a pulse."

"Agreed." He was glad she'd thought of it. Lammers had said "body," and he'd taken her word for it. "Can I borrow your knife?" He took latex gloves from his shoulder bag and pulled them on.

Evans handed him a utility blade. "He's male and somewhere between twenty-five and thirty."

Jackson needed to see his ID. "Have you got a blanket in your car?"

"Be right back."

She took off running across the intersection. A pang of jealousy squeezed his chest. He would love to have her energy and fitness. With his weird fibrotic disease, he wasn't likely to ever be in great shape again. At least the second surgery had cut back the growth and eased his pain—again.

While Evans was gone, Jackson scanned the ground with his flashlight. Bits of roadside trash, but no blood and no weapons.

"I found this," Durham said, trailing after him. "It was beside the road, near where the body was." He held out an evidence bag with a crumpled plastic water bottle.

Jackson tucked it into his shoulder bag. The crime lab would test the disposable bottle for prints and send it to the state lab for DNA analysis. If the killer had tossed it—and they found him or her—the evidence would put the perp at the scene.

Evans jogged back up. "I have this space blanket." As she unfolded it, the paper-thin shiny material glinted in the moonlight. "You want it next to the body, I assume."

"Yeah, we'll transfer him over." The idea was to catch anything that might fall off the plastic when he cut it open. A piece of hair, a strand of fabric, or even dirt from the perp's yard. They needed any and all forensic evidence.

When he and Evans had the blanket smoothed out, patrol officers joined them on both ends of the plastic bundle. Nobody was stupid enough to suggest Evans step aside. Even with four people, the weight was substantial. Jackson guessed the victim was at least his size, six-feet and two-hundred pounds, but most likely bigger. Not an easy person to overpower. He tried not to jump to conclusions. But with young male deaths, the motive was usually drugs or love gone wrong. Occasionally, they lost their lives in a fit of rage over something stupid like a video game or bad driving.

"Can I take the bungee cords off?" Evans sounded eager as usual.

"Just unhook them and leave them in place." He planned to close the whole thing back up for the ME to transport. With any luck, he hoped to find a lead and get out of there before the medical examiner showed up.

Evans made quick work of the cords. Jackson squatted, and his incision sent a shock of pain into his groin. He paused and took a quick breath before sliding the blade into the first layer of plastic. He sliced as far as he could, scooted to cut the bottom half, then repeated the process with the second layer of plastic. As the body was exposed, the smell of blood wafted up, warm, rusty, and dank—but no scent of decomposing flesh. That meant their window of opportunity to find and apprehend the killer was still open.

The holes in the victim's chest seemed like obvious buckshot wounds, probably at close range. While Evans shone her flashlight on the area, Jackson touched a gloved fingertip to the dark T-shirt. Wet blood pooled on the latex.

"He hasn't been dead long," Evans commented.

Jackson made himself look at the man's face. Anglo, moderately attractive, but not anyone he recognized as a known criminal. "Let's search his jeans for a wallet."

They each worked a side but came up empty-handed. Jackson swore under his breath. Another victim with no identification.

"Photos of his face," Evans announced.

After they both took pictures, Jackson looked up at the patrol officers. "Get his image on your phones, then start canvassing this area. Identifying him is our priority."

The crunch of tires on gravel made them all turn. A vehicle had pulled into the area next to where the driver/witness sat. A sheriff's department car. A man in a hat climbed out and hurried over. Short and heavyset, he breathed hard. "Deputy Stockton." He sized up the group and extended a hand to Jackson, who introduced himself.

"Why wasn't the county called?" Stockton wanted to know. "This side of Greenhill is our jurisdiction."

Jackson had expected the issue to come up. "Dispatch made the decision. I assume it's because this corner is actually within the city's boundaries." He kept his tone casual. "The line does a funny little jog to include this property."

"Huh." The deputy sounded skeptical. "That doesn't make sense."

"Except"—Jackson pointed at a boarded-over building at the edge of the lot—"that used to be a thriving gas station and store, back when there was nothing else out here. I'm sure the city wanted to keep the property tax revenue."

The deputy didn't look happy, but nodded anyway. "What have we got? And how can I help?"

"We need to ID the victim. So get photos of his face and send them out to your people."

Stockton leaned sideways to look behind Jackson at the body. "Is that plastic? Was he wrapped and dropped?"

"We don't know yet, but our working theory is that he rolled out of the back of a truck."

"I'll be damned. I wonder if the driver was on his way to the dump." The deputy looked relieved. *Apparently, it wasn't a case he actually wanted.*

Evans cut in. "I doubt it. Going through town would be a risk. The perp was likely coming from the city, headed to a quiet spot out here to dump or bury him."

After a moment, Jackson broke the silence. "Let's get on it. We need a name."

Chapter 4

Wednesday, September 18, 5:45 a.m.
Jackson woke to a tiny finger tapping his face.

"Daddy!"

"What?" He bolted upright, and so did Kera.

Benjie stood by the bed, distressed but not in tears. The boy never cried. "I had a bad dream. Then I woke up and Micah was gone."

Kera bolted out of bed, wearing only a long T-shirt, and ran toward the boys' shared room. Jackson shook the fog out of his head, forced himself to stand, and glanced at the clock. He'd only had two hours of sleep—after spending half the night driving around rural roads, knocking on doors and showing the victim's photo. The effort had netted nothing except a blinding headache this morning. But he still had to function. He bent down and kissed Benjie's forehead. "I'm sure Micah is around here somewhere. Thanks for caring."

Out in the hall, he heard Kera sigh with relief when she discovered her grandson sleeping on the couch in the family room. Jackson shuffled to the kitchen and started a full pot of coffee. He would drink half now and take the rest with him. Today would be long and likely frustrating.

While the java brewed, he dressed for work and chatted with Benjie, who tended to follow him around. Back in the kitchen, Jackson poured a cup of coffee and asked the boy what he wanted for breakfast.

"Avocado toast. Whole wheat, please."

"What?" Jackson laughed. "Are you messing with me?"

"No, it's delicious." Benjie grinned. "I had it at daycare."

"We don't have avocados."

"Yes we do." The boy pointed to a bowl on the counter.

Jackson rolled his eyes. He loved the kid, but he didn't have time for this. Micah wandered into the kitchen, rubbing his eyes. "I want cereal."

That, he could handle. Jackson pulled out the milk, gulped a mouthful of coffee, and silently pleaded with Kera to relieve him.

As he poured two bowls of cereal, Benjie crossed his arms. "I don't want that. Too much sugar."

Kera finally came in, fully dressed and hiding a smile.

"What's so funny?"

"I wanted to watch you make avocado toast."

"I have the skills, just not the time." Jackson abandoned the breakfast project and poured a thermos of coffee. "I have to go." He hugged everyone and headed for the bedroom to retrieve his weapon. As he hurried toward the front door, Kera called out, "Would you put the wet clothes in the dryer, please?" Jackson ignored the request, suppressed his guilt, and kept moving. His team was probably already en route to work.

In his cubicle, he booted up his computer and enjoyed a moment of silence. Even when the second floor filled with detectives and technicians, the space would still be quieter than his home. After skimming through his emails, Jackson opened the department's database and accessed the new facial-recognition software. From inside the program, he loaded the victim's image and started the search.

One partial match surfaced. The two men had similarly shaped faces, particularly their noses. But the ex-con in the database was older than the victim, and the guy they'd found dumped in the road had a scar on his chin.

Repressing a sigh, Jackson opened Facebook.

"I'll do the social media search." Evans poked her head into his cube. "I know how much you hate it." As she spoke, she stepped next to him and put a hand on his shoulder.

Her touch sent a jolt through his body. "Uh, thanks. I'll call the media."

"Are we getting any help with this one? Or meeting to discuss?"

"Not yet. We need an ID first."

"I'm on it." She headed next door to her own workspace.

Jackson picked up his cell and called a local TV station. Five rings later, he had to leave a message asking for a callback. He tried a second media company with a similar result. The on-air people changed so often, he never bothered to get to know them, and he certainly didn't have their personal phone numbers. So he stared at a contact labeled *Sophie Speranza* and braced himself. His caffeine hadn't fully kicked in, and the reporter could be a little intense.

She picked up after two rings. "Hey, Jackson. I'm not even at work yet, so this must be important." A thud in the background, followed by Sophie's sharp intake of breath. "Shit! I just stubbed my toe on the bedpost."

He waited a moment for her to settle down. But now he was visualizing her bed and Jasmine Parker climbing out of it. A while back, he'd discovered they were romantically involved, and he'd had to warn Parker, a crime-scene technician, about sharing confidential information with the press. She'd given him an icy stare, rolled her eyes, and gone back to work. A few days later, Parker had been promoted.

"I need a favor," Jackson said, wanting to wrap up the call already.

"What is it? Do you have a new case?" Sophie sounded like she was still in pain.

"Yes. A gunshot victim with no ID. I need help identifying him."

"Again? Are criminals actually getting smarter?"

"Maybe. I'll email you his image in a minute."

"Where was he shot? I mean the location."

"We don't know."

"You gotta give me something."

"The body was found in the road just off Highway 126. That's all I know." Mostly true. Should he give her details? Could it help his investigation?

"What are you holding back?"

Jackson mulled it over a moment longer. What if someone had seen the black roll in the back of a neighbor's truck and didn't know it was a body? He decided he had nothing to lose. "The victim was wrapped in plastic and likely shot somewhere else."

"Interesting! So he was being transported?"

"We don't know for sure."

"Time of death?"

"Sometime last evening." He still hadn't spoken to Gunderson, but that outreach was next. "I have to go." Jackson ended the call and rang the medical examiner. The old man didn't answer, so he left a message: "Hey, it's Jackson. I need a TOD on the John Doe victim and an autopsy time. Sooner is better, of course."

Even though they hadn't had a homicide in a while, the ME still had to attend every death that occurred: drug overdoses, accidents at home, vehicle-crash victims. Most people didn't get a full autopsy, but the poor guy looked at dead bodies every day. Jackson tried to keep that in mind when Gunderson called back a few minutes later.

"What the hell, Jackson? You cut open the plastic, scattered the trace evidence, then left the damn scene before I could get there." His voice sounded raw, like a man who hadn't been awake long enough to wet his throat.

"Sorry, but I had to search for his wallet. And we were careful to collect the trace."

"So who is he?"

"We don't know yet. But I'm hoping his clothes or his autopsy will give us something to go on."

"The post is scheduled for three this afternoon. I sent his clothes to the crime lab, so talk to them. Right now, I have to sleep for another hour." The ME was off the line.

Jackson added *talk to crime lab* to his to-do list. But it was too early to make that visit. The technicians needed time to process everything, and it wasn't likely that tracking down the origin of a pair of jeans would produce a lead. They needed someone in the public to recognize their victim and give them a name. Until then, he felt almost useless.

Chapter 5

Wednesday, 5:45 a.m.

The hot-air balloon lifted off the ground, giving Agent Jamie Dallas a rush of excitement. Not exactly the adrenaline burst she experienced when skydiving or zip-lining, but still glorious—and this excursion would last longer. As the balloon drifted higher and higher, her grin widened. She loved seeing the massive city below, laid out like a grid, shrinking slowly down to model-scale size. The wide-open blue sky drifted with clouds at eye level, and a hawk soared by.

The pilot changed directions and headed north, and soon she spotted hills, canyons, and square plots of land below. As the city faded into the distance, an eerie silence engulfed them. Even the wind quieted, and all she could hear was her own pulse.

Her heart filled with joy, and for a moment she forgot everything else, including the other people on the flight. She loved this sensation so much. Feeling like a bird who could fly anywhere, free from restrictions or planned routes. Above and away from everything, especially the desk she'd been stuck at for a while. Away from the crime and fear and trauma she encountered on her job every day.

The excursion was an early morning birthday gift to

herself, and she thought she might make it a yearly tradition. The only thing that would have made it better was sharing it with Cameron, who was in Flagstaff working. She would see him for a late dinner tonight after he drove down. She looked forward to wrapping up this perfect day with amazing sex, a great way to say goodbye to her twenties.

Two hours later, Dallas strode into the Phoenix FBI office, feeling both at home and restless at the same time. Sliding into her desk chair, she opened her computer and scanned the bureau's newsfeed. Upstairs, a special team of agents and analysts stared at a roomful of monitors, watching around-the-clock for breaking events across the nation. Still, taking America's crime pulse was also her first responsibility. Nothing eye-popping stood out. Politics had so consumed the citizenry that, except for hate crimes, the rate of federal offenses had actually dropped.

But criminals never took breaks, so Dallas grudgingly opened a report she'd started about a local fraud ring run by a sixty-two-year-old woman with a gift for real estate scams. The grifter preyed on out-of-town seniors looking to buy winter homes in the area. Dallas had posed as a sketchy realtor to help bust the scammers. The assignment had taken her out of the office, but not out of town. And not deep enough undercover to suit her. She loved taking on a whole new persona to penetrate deep into a criminal ring. Just thinking about the risk sent a surge of energy through her body.

Her desk phone rang, startling her. Line one, her new boss. She picked up. "Good morning, sir."

"Come to my office, please. I have a high-priority assignment for you."

Yes! Dallas jumped up, adrenaline pulsing again. She hustled upstairs to the corner office where Special Agent Radner ran their division. Notepad in hand, she hurried through the open door. Behind his desk, Radner hunched forward, masking the full size of his impressive frame. His gray kinky hair, cut close to the scalp, contrasted with his dark skin tone, and his face was sweet to look at. She repressed a surge of sexual attraction and sat down. "What have you got for me?"

"An undercover job in Vancouver. A string of roofie rapes near the state university campus."

"You want me to work as bait." The risk didn't bother her, but the lack of challenge did.

"You're exactly his type." Radner paused and gave her a small smile. "Blonde, blue-eyed, and attractive. You don't even have to change your looks."

Dallas nodded, trying to hide her disappointment. Like any good actress, she liked changing her appearance. That was part of the fun. So was changing her name, location, and personality. When she'd first taken acting classes in high school, she would have laughed at the idea that she would end up in law enforcement. Not with *her* sketchy parents. But here she was. "What do we know about the suspect?"

"Two of the earlier victims recall talking to a guy who looked thirty. They think he was dark blond and a little heavyset. But others, assaulted later, said he might have brownish hair but bald in front. So there could be two assailants."

"Or maybe he's changing his looks." Making her job harder. "Also, dark blond and brownish could be the same color. And if the women were drugged, they might not remember the perp at all, maybe just the guy they talked to right before."

Agent Radner pushed a folder across the desk. "Six sexual assault reports are in the file, plus a list of sexual predators in the Vancouver area. I've also submitted a subpoena to the university for a list of all their male students. Once we have it, our analysts will round up photos and sort the names along any demographic you ask for."

"Excellent. Who's my local contact?"

"I don't know yet, but someone will text your burner phone after you arrive in Vancouver."

"My new alias?"

"Amber Davison. Since you're not going in deep, the UC team is generating a fake ID this time. You can pick it up on your way out today."

Her excitement mounted. When she went deep undercover, she had to wait for the DMV to create a real driver's license and for the undercover team to generate background files such as school records, social media pages, and an appropriate resume. Not this time. "When do I leave?"

"As soon as you wrap up your personal obligations. You might be gone two weeks or two months. The Vancouver police haven't had any luck tracking this perp, so we know he's careful." Her boss paused for a moment. "He's also escalating. The last victim woke up in his car with the engine running. She bolted but was too panicked to get a description or plate number."

"You think he was trying to kidnap her?"

"Possibly."

"I'll be careful."

"And you'll wear a tracker."

"Of course." Dallas started to get up. "I'll book a flight for the morning."

"Wait. There's more."

An unexpected wave of apprehension hit her as she sat back down.

"We recently found a new group of online incels with disturbingly violent rhetoric. I need you to set up a profile and get inside. Maybe we'll spot our perp."

The assignment both excited and repulsed her. She'd read enough *involuntary celibate* rants to know how angry and irrational their attitudes were. "What's the URL?"

"It's in your folder; the website is called Not Normal."

Dallas coughed up a harsh laugh. "No kidding. At least they have some self-awareness."

Radner shook his head. "Not really. They call everyone else—meaning those of us having sex—*normies*. But they take no responsibility for their own lack thereof. They blame women for apparently failing to fulfill their social obligation to provide sex." Her boss looked perplexed and amused at the same time. "But you probably are aware of all this."

"I've done some reading on the topic. What else do we know about the members?"

"Their digital fingerprints come from all over the country. But some are probably tech savvy enough to use VPNs or proxy servers." Radner locked eyes with her, his long years on the job making his brow wrinkled. "There's also a lot of overlap with white supremacist organizations, so you have to assume anyone from the group is carrying."

"Got it." Dallas squirmed, eager to get started. "Anything else?"

"Don't meet anyone without backup." Agent Radner stood, signaling she should too. "Don't worry much about blowing your cover. This isn't an organized crime ring. Just a lone sexual predator."

Dallas nodded. But as she walked out, doubts set in. What if the perp didn't work alone? What if he had help and support from the group? This sting might be more dangerous than they realized.

Chapter 6

Wednesday, 10:35 a.m.

Still at his desk, Jackson made a to-do list: *clothes/bullets/fingerprints, check with county/state, autopsy.* Pretty short for a murder investigation. But until he knew who the man was—and could access his financial and social records—determining a motive would be impossible.

He called the crime lab and asked to talk to Joe Berloni, the senior tech who processed most of the physical evidence from homicides. It took forever to get him on the line. As he waited, Jackson added to his list and wondered how Evans was doing with the Facebook search.

"Hey, Jackson." Joe's voice boomed in his ear. "I've only had a few hours on this case today, so I don't have much yet."

"I know it's early, but I need an ID."

"Sorry, but the dead man's fingerprints are not in the database."

"Well, crap. I'm not sure where else to look."

"Maybe a body of water."

Interesting. "Tell me more."

"The victim's boots are damp, and they had tiny clumps of *fontinalis*, a moss that grows around lakes and ponds."

"Can you narrow that down?"

"Sorry, but no."

"Maybe he liked to fish. Or canoe." Jackson jotted down the note out of habit. "Anything else?"

"Classic 501 jeans, waist 32, length 34. And he had a speck of moss on the rolled cuff of his jeans."

"What about his pockets?" Jackson had searched them for a wallet or driver's license, but Joe would have turned them inside out and studied the cloth under a microscope.

"Nothing helpful. Just a little tobacco powder."

"So he smoked."

"It's more likely chew, but I haven't looked at it chemically yet."

Jackson took more notes. "At least we know something."

"Do you want me to track down where the boots were manufactured?"

"Only when you have time." The info would have been more important if they were dealing with shoes or prints left by the killer. Jackson still hoped to ID the victim long before the technician could complete such an exhaustive search. "Anything on the gun or ammo yet?"

"I'm still waiting for Gunderson to send over any buckshot he found in the body."

"But you're sure the wounds were made with a shotgun?"

"Definitely."

"Thanks, Joe. Call me if you have any updates."

They both clicked off, and Jackson called the Lane County Sheriff's office. A deputy had been at the scene, but they still needed a desk person to search their files for someone resembling the victim and/or a similar crime. Jackson tried to get the sheriff himself on the line but had to settle for a deputy, who said he'd get right on it. After a call to the state police with the same request, Jackson checked the time. He still had an hour before the autopsy.

He stood and stretched, going easy to protect his scar. More accurately, to protect himself from the pain of abusing the wound. Grabbing his cold coffee, he stepped out of his cube and walked around to Evans' space.

"Hey, any luck with Facebook?"

"No." She spun to face him, her brow creased. *She was still lovely in her light-blue blouse.* Evans shrugged. "Without a name, it feels pretty pointless. I've searched using the general area where the body was found, and I've scanned through hundreds of images of Eugene men. I found two guys who look kinda like our victim, but they're both alive and well."

"Let me see. I'd settle for finding a relative."

"Not these guys." Evans loaded a page and scooted sideways.

Jackson stepped up to her monitor. The man showing was in his late forties. Likely too old to be a brother and too young to be John Doe's father. "Did you check his family members?"

"Of course." She gave him a slight smile. "They're all in Kansas."

"And the other guy you found?"

Evans reached over, clicked the back arrow twice, and moved aside.

A pleasant fruit scent wafted from her hair. Jackson did his best to ignore it.

The second profile image was a better match age-wise, but his nose was bigger and his chin too narrow. Jackson stepped back. "Thanks for trying. I talked to Joe, and we know our victim was recently near a pond or lake, likely chews tobacco, and was killed with a shotgun."

She didn't bother to take notes. "So he and the killer are both rural folks."

"Seems that way. We only ended up with this case because the idiot lost the body inside a corner of our boundary."

Evans tapped her desk. "It would help if our vic had a tattoo or birthmark we could track down."

"I'm headed to the autopsy this afternoon, so it's still a possibility." He started to walk away.

"Oh, hey," she called. "We need to post his image on the department's Facebook page. Some people actually follow us." Evans let out a laugh. "Mostly old paranoid types and families of criminals, but still, we can ask them to share the picture to the broader community."

"Great idea. Will you contact our PR person too?"

"I'm on it."

Chapter 7

Wednesday, 10:55 a.m.

After dropping the boys at preschool, Kera Kollmorgan drove to the fertility clinic, parked, and sat in her car for a few minutes. Overwhelmed with grief and worry, she didn't know if she could function. Nate, her beautiful son, had been killed in a senseless war. And his baby boy, Micah, looked so much like him it hurt her heart. Every damn day. Her parents were gone too. Some days, she felt so alone she wanted to die.

Now that she and Jackson were finally living together, he seemed distant and drifting away. She knew it was her fault for being gone so long to take care of her dying parents. Dear god, she missed them. Another tidal wave of sadness washed over her, and she let herself cry for a few minutes.

"Okay, girl. That's enough. You have stuff to do." Kera wiped the mascara from under her eyes and climbed from the car. Patients counted on her. The boys counted on her. Jackson did too, in his own aloof way.

As she walked into the clinic lobby, she straightened her shoulders, noting how different the space was from Planned Parenthood's. Here, they had plush carpeting, soft chairs, and expensive art on the walls. Not to mention the quiet. Only a single person waited to be seen. At the sound of Kera's footsteps, the tall woman jumped up and hurried over.

Erica. A fertility patient she'd worked with months ago. Kera struggled to remember her last name. "Hi Erica. How are you?"

"Worried. Can we talk in private?"

"Of course." They moved toward the entry to the exam rooms. Kera waved her security card, waited for the click, then held the door open.

The hum of refrigerators and soft conversations seeped into the hall as they walked to the back. When they were seated in a counseling room, Erica burst into tears. Kera reached over and held her hand while she cried. This had to be about a baby. That was the business she was in now. Helping women get pregnant instead of preventing it. She steeled herself. This patient needed her to be calm and resourceful.

Finally Erica got control. "Sorry. I think I've been holding that in for a while."

"It's all right. Tell me what's going on."

"My surrogate isn't answering my calls or texts. I'm worried that she's planning to keep the baby."

Oh dear. She remembered now. Erica produced eggs, but couldn't carry a fetus to term. So she'd had one of her embryos implanted into a surrogate. Kera could visualize the other woman. Small, dark-haired, and pretty. But she hadn't seen her in awhile. "When did you last hear from her?"

"We talked three weeks ago. I try not to be overly involved or annoying, but I check in with her every two weeks. When I called last Friday, she didn't respond. I've been trying to reach her since. Will you try? She might answer if the call comes from the clinic."

"Sure." Kera reached for the conference-style phone in the middle of the table and pulled it toward them. "Remind me of her name, please."

"Bettina Rios."

She should have remembered, but grief seemed to have punched holes in her brain. "Would you key in her number?"

Erica tapped the buttons, her hands shaking.

The repeated ringing gave Kera a sick feeling. But it didn't necessarily mean anything. At the prompt, she left a message: "Hi Bettina. It's Kera Kollmorgan from the Fertility Support Center. Would you please give me a call?"

Erica bit her lip. "I went by her house yesterday. Her car was there, but she didn't answer."

"You're not supposed to do that. How do you know her address?"

"She told me. We've become friends." Erica sucked in a breath. "Or I thought we had."

The whole situation felt beyond Kera's expertise. She was just a nurse who gave fertility shots and monitored patients' health stats. "I'm wondering if you should contact the police. They can check on Bettina."

"Isn't your husband a detective? I think you mentioned that once."

Kera didn't correct her assumption about marriage. "Yeah, but Jackson handles violent crimes, not missing people."

Erica was silent for a minute.

A pang of fear sparked in Kera's chest. "Do you think something bad happened to Bettina?"

"I don't know." Erica started to cry again. "Either that or she disappeared on purpose with my child. Would you ask Jackson to check this out for me? Please?"

The last thing he needed. "You should go into the department and file a missing-person report."

Erica bit her lip again. "I don't expect them to take me seriously. I'm not Bettina's co-worker or sister or neighbor. And the whole surrogacy thing? People are so uncomfortable with it. Men especially. I don't want to have to explain this to an insensitive, bully-type guy in a uniform."

Kera noticed Erica's skin color for the first time. She was likely mixed-race with some African American. Was she afraid of police officers? Even in Eugene? "Okay. I'll ask Jackson to look into this. But I suspect everything will turn out fine. If Bettina calls me back, I'll find out what's going on and let you know right away."

Chapter 8

Wednesday, 2:55 p.m.

As he took the elevator down to the basement of the old hospital, Jackson's stomach rumbled. He'd skipped lunch because he knew after years of attending autopsies that a full stomach in the morgue was not a good idea. Nicknamed Surgery Ten by insiders, the space was no bigger than a living room. He knocked once and stepped inside. Even without natural light, the combination of stainless steel and intense lighting made him blink.

Rudolph Konrad, the pathologist who performed the autopsies, nodded at him. "Gown up and we'll get started."

"Without the ME?" Jackson reached for a blue paper gown.

"Gunderson is resting after being up all night, prepping the body. Be glad. He sounded quite cranky." A smile flickered on Konrad's face.

Were those wrinkles around his eyes? Jackson suppressed his own grin. The chubby-cheeked pathologist was finally looking more his age.

"He also said you had insisted I conduct the post today." Konrad pulled over a wheeled tray loaded with shiny miniature tools. "Fortunately, my schedule could accommodate the rush."

"Thanks." Jackson tied a mask around his face and moved toward the table. The plastic had been removed, and the man's body lay bare and exposed. Despite a lack of blood, his skin looked as though he'd spent time in the sun. It was also marked by faded-purple spots everywhere. *Good grief! Had he been tortured?* "Are those scars?"

"Yes."

"Cigarette burns?"

"No. Too superficial. But they are the result of slow-healing scabs." Konrad scanned the body, quiet for a moment. Finally he said, "Taking into account his skin color and the parasites present in his blood, I speculate that this man spent a lot of time in a tropical environment." With gloved fingers, the pathologist squeezed one of the purple scars. "I think these might have been insect bites that got infected years ago."

Oh hell. The victim might not even be a US citizen. Or have any paperwork. Or local contacts. Maybe he was a drug smuggler. Or a human trafficker. A deep worry settled into Jackson's empty stomach. This case might turn out to be one of the few he couldn't solve. Staying to watch the guy's chest be cut open wouldn't change that. "Have we determined a time of death?"

"Last evening, sometime between seven and nine." As he talked, the pathologist checked between the corpse's toes.

So the victim had been shot only a few hours before he landed on the road. "Do we know the caliber of the shotgun?"

Konrad kept searching the man's skin. "Most likely a twelve gauge. He has a chest cavity full of buckshot wounds from a relatively close range. Ten feet or less." The pathologist glanced up, looking over the top of his glasses. "I'm sure I'll find a pellet or two stuck under the skin of his back—when I get to that point in the process."

Jackson tried to suppress his impatience, but couldn't. "Any evidence that he's a drug runner?"

Konrad gave a small shake of his head, clearly annoyed. "I'm just getting started. Are you in a hurry?"

"Yes. Sorry. But I need to know who he is, and most of this process won't likely help me."

"Then go. I'll send you my report."

Jackson needed to know something first. "Will you do a cavity search, please?"

Konrad stared for a long moment. Doing it now would mess up his usual sequence. "All right."

"Thanks."

Jackson glanced away while the pathologist probed the victim's anus. He looked back in time to see him pull out a tiny piece of blue plastic, or maybe rubber.

"This looks like a fragment of a heavy-duty balloon, the type used by drug mules. But I won't know for sure until I examine it under a scope." Konrad locked eyes with him again. "Does that help?"

Feeling guilty, Jackson had to admit he didn't really know.

Konrad transferred the evidence onto a glass slide. "I examined the victim's mouth before you arrived and found that his teeth are quite decayed. That's consistent with heavy drug use, especially methamphetamines."

"Good to know." But a lot of people used meth, so it didn't narrow down his identity. "One more question, then I have to go."

Konrad sighed. "Yes?"

"Does he have any tattoos that I can't see from here?"

"Just one." The pathologist leaned in to examine the dead man's chest from a few inches away. "I believe this ink was shaped like a heart, but buckshot pellets rather destroyed it."

"Thanks. That might be helpful." Jackson stepped back, shed his protective clothing, and hurried out. If he didn't have an ID by the end of the day, he would contact the FBI for help.

Chapter 9

Wednesday, 5:25 p.m.

Dallas rushed into her apartment, mentally working through her task list. She'd accomplished most of the main chores over the phone at work. Airline tickets purchased, a hotel room leased in Vancouver, and her landlord notified. The physical logistics were easy too. She had no pets or plants to worry about, and all her bills were on auto-pay.

Her furnishings were minimalist as well, and that suited both her personal tastes and nomadic lifestyle. She loved adrenaline, movement, freedom . . . and hated clutter, repetition, and boredom. The counseling she'd subjected herself to in college had zipped right past how she'd had to care for herself as a child because of her drug-and-alcohol-addicted parents and had zeroed in on how she'd become both detached and addicted to drama. Blah, blah, blah. At least she put her personality disorder to good use.

In the kitchen, she opened a microbrew and drank a third of it, dreading the call she still had to make. The hardest part of this whole thing was telling Cameron she was leaving town again. She'd texted him earlier to cancel their dinner plans, and he wasn't too happy. He wanted her to give up undercover work, but she couldn't do that. Not yet. Not until she found another way to keep from getting bored out of her mind—while still making money. She would pack first. Give herself time to formulate the right words. Maybe offer to spend time in Flagstaff after she wrapped up her assignment.

In the hall closet, she retrieved her purple luggage, which seemed more appropriate for a college student than the charcoal set. Packing went quickly. She loaded all her favorite clothes, plus a few lightweight jackets, then pulled together all her bathroom stuff. In the mirror, she stared at her long blonde hair, wishing she could cut and dye it again. Maybe a light strawberry rinse. She kept it her natural color when she was in the office, because her looks landed her undercover gigs. The leaders at the bureau were still men. So were most criminals.

Her track record on assignments was excellent. She'd stopped a dangerous doomsday cult, exposed a corporate saboteur in the pharma industry, and even brought down a top-brass traitor in their own ranks. But for women, performance was never enough. They had to look good and/or latch onto the right men in power. Dallas didn't mind engaging in semi-sexual encounters with perps and informants to get information that would land them in prison, but she never used her body to gain status. The men who could promote her could also blacklist her. She would never give anyone that much power in a relationship.

Done with her list, she ate a salad and a chocolate truffle for dinner, then put in her earpiece to call Cameron.

He answered with his usual, "Hey, babe," and his deep honey voice sent a jolt to her sexy parts. It had been too long. But with Cameron, anything more than a few days made her feel deprived. They'd dated in high school—the only time she'd ever felt *in love*—then reconnected earlier this year when she'd gone home to see her dying father.

"Hey, Cam. I wish you were here right now. My body really misses you."

"Just your body?"

"My stomach too. You make the best damn tacos." Dallas laughed. She loved Cameron in her own way, but she was still uncomfortable expressing it. "All that will have to wait. I'm flying out on assignment tomorrow."

He was silent so long it worried her.

"Don't freak out. It's an easy gig that shouldn't take long."

"What do you mean by *easy*?"

"I'm not going in deep this time. I just have to hang out around a college campus for a while."

"Let me guess. You'll be bait for a sting."

"Something like that."

"I wish you would quit this kind of work."

More silence. They'd had this conversation after her last deep-cover role, which had almost gotten her killed, but she wasn't ready to settle into deskwork. Far from it. She still wanted to join the CIA and work overseas. But intelligence work was a relationship killer. So she usually broke up with the guy she was dating before leaving on a new assignment. Cameron was different.

"Like I said, it's not deep cover. So if the sting takes a while, I can make trips home. You'll probably see me as much as you usually do." *Maybe.*

"Can I drive down tonight? I need to be with you, and I don't want to miss your birthday entirely."

"So tempting. But no, I have work to do."

"If I lived in Phoenix, you could squeeze me in more often."

She started to make a sexual joke, then realized he was feeling too serious for it. The poor guy really wanted to sell his brewery in Flagstaff and settle down with her in Phoenix. Was it time to break up with him? The thought gave her unexpected anxiety.

"I'll be in touch, I promise. And I'll fly out to see you as soon as I can. Love you." She got off the phone before he could make a big deal of her saying it. She'd tried to sound casual, the way she would with a friend. Although she didn't really have any real friends, except her hairdresser. Her job was too strange and secretive. Cameron wasn't supposed to know she worked undercover, but after almost dying, she'd had a weak moment and told him—and regretted it ever since.

Her phone pinged, and she glanced down. A text from Cam: *I love you too!*

Oh hell. Why had she opened that door?

Dallas let it go, grabbed her laptop, and did a quick glance at her favorite news sites. She checked her work email and her current Yahoo account, but there were no new messages. She didn't have any social media accounts to peruse, except for one phony Facebook profile, because her career required her to stay in the shadows. She closed the laptop and tucked it under the couch. Time to say goodbye to Jamie Dallas for a while. The black PC the bureau had provided sat on her coffee table, waiting. First she had to create a profile that couldn't be traced to Phoenix.

She pulled a key out of a secret compartment in her bathroom and unlocked the small second bedroom at the end of the hall. A desk at the back wall held a computer and server. The space also contained a gun safe and a trunk filled with purses, backpacks, jackets, and pants—that all had hidden pockets.

Dallas sat down at the computer and accessed a proxy

server in Croatia. From there, she loaded Facebook and set up a new account, using the name James Barton. He sounded white and midwestern, like he might be from Dayton, Ohio. From her image file—supplied by the bureau—she chose a guy in his late twenties with short ash-blond hair and acne. To fill out the personal-photo section, she uploaded a dozen shots of a mangy sweet-faced dog and a few camping-by-the-river pictures.

Her first post as James Barton laid the groundwork: *Im back! But still pissed at FB for not helping me recovr my old profile. fucking hacker! so friend me and get this party started.*

She hoped that would explain Barton's lack of online history. Just in case the Not Normal moderator decided to check it. She'd glanced at the site earlier out of curiosity but hadn't had time to study it yet. She keyed in the URL, and the landing page loaded. The crude design and tone jarred her. No thought had been given to aesthetics, and the subtitle said it all: *For guys who can't get laid and hate the women who say no.* A narrow column on the right had links to a variety of other pages, and the main space listed titles of forum topics: *Working with Bitches, Rejection and Revenge, Favorite Porn Violence* . . . and more like it.

She hadn't even started on the personal comments.

Dallas clicked the top thread, and a dialogue box opened: *New Here? Join if you want to participate.*

Another link took her to an application page, where she spent twenty careful minutes filling out a profile and a request to join. She wouldn't be allowed to post or communicate with others in the network until she did. For a photo, she uploaded a close-up of the dog she'd used on FB. The other users on the site hadn't posted their real images either, just a lot of weird stuff. Not expecting a response for days, she grabbed her favorite undercover purse and headed back to the living room and the PC laptop.

After reading a couple of articles about the incel world, including examples of their posts, she went to the fridge for another beer. The lingo alone would take some getting used to. Women were *fembots* and *sluttybitches.* That was nothing compared to the dark and disturbing shit these men—reportedly in the tens of thousands—casually tossed around. Repulsive complaints about girls never taking showers and being unsanitary. Offhand remarks about throwing acid in women's faces. Calls for harsh Sharia law to keep them under control. That startled her.

According to her research, most incels were white men who lived in the US or Europe. The overall message screamed that females weren't really people, just sexual objects that fell into simple categories: Attractive or dogs. Sluts or prudes. Worthy of life or not.

That last mode of thought terrified her. If a woman wasn't fuckable, for whatever reason, she had no right to exist. Racist incels were already conducting mass shootings and bombings to express their hatred for nonwhites. What if others decided to target large gatherings of women next?

Disgusted, Dallas downed a slug of her favorite brew, one of Cam's dark creations. Beer alone might not be strong enough to get her through this. To blend in, she had to immerse herself in their world, but it was too early in the gig to get into survival mode.

She checked the new Yahoo account she'd given as her email address, and a message from *TribalDragon* sat at the top. She opened it, pleased to discover that James Barton was now welcome in the dark, misogynistic Not Normal world. She tapped the link to the site and opened the thread at the top of the page, an angry screed about working for female bosses. Dallas skimmed through and got quickly to the comments.

From *JungleBoy*: *Why r woman bosses so bitchy? & what the hell is rong with tanktops? Nobody fuckin sees me. #bitchybosses #manhoodatrisk*

TribalDragon: *If bulging pecs freak her out start wearing tight shorts and show your dick instead. #Reclaimmanhood*

The next comment came from a charmer named *Mas7erD3bator*: *Tie the shirt around her neck and make her suck your cock!*

Dallas wanted to punch them all in the face. But she had to let her anger go and embrace theirs—at least on the surface, so she could earn their trust. She clicked the comment button, and her new persona appeared at the top of a box: *bi*chgirlhater.* She'd used the asterisk in case someone else had taken the avatar or on the slight chance the site screened for profanity in usernames. *Hah!* A laughable thought.

Submerging herself into the role, she posted her first comment in the incelosphere: *My last boss made me bring her coffee so I spit in it everyday. #servesyourightbitch*

She sat back, finished her beer, and reminded herself of why she was doing this. One of the bastards on this site was drugging and raping women in Vancouver, and she intended to bring him down.

Chapter 10

Wednesday, 6:15 p.m.
Jackson heated leftover pizza in the microwave, then sat to watch the news. Another thing he loved about the new department. They'd moved more than a year ago, but after decades in the crowded old building he still found things to appreciate in the new one. Space and natural light being foremost. The break room TV, which he'd never watched before, was pretty cool too. His only interest now was seeing how the station handled their report about the unidentified dead guy.

The newscaster was young enough to be fresh out of college, but she'd be gone—off to a bigger media market—in six months or a year, like they all were. The local stations probably paid the men better, explaining why they stuck around longer. The newswoman mentioned the body at the top of her report, injecting a breathy *can-you-believe-this?* tone. She warned viewers the image might be disturbing before the station displayed the victim's face, leaving it in the corner for the rest of her brief report.

"Police haven't speculated about why the gunshot victim was wrapped in plastic or in the middle of the road, but we'll update you when we know more. Meanwhile, if you recognize this man, please call the number on the screen."

That was it. He hoped the other local station gave it a little more time. Still, the image was finally out there for the public to see. Someone had to know this guy . . . unless he'd just been passing through with drugs or other illegal goods.

Jackson considered going home for a while. After the autopsy, he'd met briefly with Schak and Evans to share the information, then told them both to take a break and get some sleep while they could. He knew Evans would keep working, so he should too . . . but he had a family.

As he stood, his phone rang. *Kera.* He took the call and sat back down, glad the break room was empty. "Hey, sweetie. Sorry, I'm working late."

"I miss you." A pause. "Did you get dinner?"

"Leftover pizza from Schak's lunch."

"He shared his pizza?" She sounded genuinely surprised.

Jackson laughed. "No, I helped myself, so I'll have to replace it."

Kera was quiet for a moment, then said softly, "I have a favor to ask."

"You want me to buy wine on my way home?"

"That too." She chuckled. "But my request is bigger than that. One of the clients at the fertility clinic seems to be missing."

A wave of apprehension rolled over him. "Has anyone filed a report?" This wasn't his territory, and most missing people turned up on their own.

"Not yet. It's a little complex."

Oh crap. He didn't need more complications. But Kera rarely asked him for anything. "What's the situation?

"The woman who reported her absence, Erica, is also a client. The missing woman, Bettina, is her surrogate."

Double crap. This was *so* outside his area of expertise.

"You mean Bettina, who's gone, is pregnant with a baby that somehow belongs to the other woman?" The parentage issues at the fertility clinic could be ridiculously complex.

"Correct. And Erica doesn't think she'll be taken seriously. She's also worried that her surrogate has taken off with her baby."

Jackson couldn't believe what he was about to ask, but it might be important. "Who's the biological mother?"

"Erica. The father is her deceased husband, a war veteran, who had his sperm frozen before he deployed."

Too much information. But Jackson understood why the widow didn't want to share this scenario with a stranger. Especially a cop, who was likely to be male. And cynical. And more concerned about *real* crime. He let out a deep sigh before he could stop himself.

"You don't have to do this." Kera's tone was sincere.

He knew better. "What exactly do you want me to do?"

"Go to Bettina's home and see if she'll come to the door. If she doesn't, maybe look around and try to determine if she's been there recently. If not, then Erica will have to report her missing."

"I'll stop by and ask questions. That's it."

"Thanks, hon. I'll text you her full name and address." Kera shifted gears. "How's your case going?"

"Not great. The victim is still unidentified and may not even be a US citizen."

"Should you turn this one over to the FBI? They have more resources."

He already wanted to, but having her suggest it irritated him. "If I don't hear from the public today, I will." Jackson's phone buzzed in his hand. "I'm getting another call. I'll see you later."

"Don't forget the wine. Love you." She clicked off.

The second line was Officer Davenport, their new public relations person.

"What have we got?"

"A possible ID for your gunshot victim. A woman called in but wouldn't identify herself. She says the dead guy's name is Carl and that she bought something from him a few weeks ago."

"That's pretty vague. What did she buy?" He suspected he knew.

"She didn't want to provide that information, so I'm assuming it was drugs."

"Most likely. Do you have her phone number?"

"Yes, but I looked it up. She called from the Lucky Clover."

Crap! The lead was almost worthless, but it was all he had.

The tavern occupied a stucco-sided building that had once been a Taco Bell. Painted green now, it sat on a busy intersection known by locals as *Four Corners*. Dozens of fast-food restaurants in the vicinity had come and gone over the decades. The drug trade and homeless population made it difficult to attract people with money or children to the area. Only bars, gas stations, and run-down motels survived—plus a strip-club or two.

As Jackson entered the Lucky Clover, the smell of rancid deep-fryer grease hit him hard. Taking shallow breaths, he moved toward the counter, hoping to escape the dark, dank atmosphere as quickly as possible. The bartender, a tall, fifty-something man, stiffened as he approached. "What do you want?" The chilly tone made Jackson wonder what he had to hide.

"I'm looking for a guy named Carl. He's about my size and in his mid-to-late twenties. Shoulder-length light-brown hair and a heart-shaped tattoo on his chest."

A woman on a barstool swung to face Jackson. "What about him?" Middle-aged with drunk eyes and flaming red-dyed hair, she slurred a little.

"I need to know his last name."

She squinted, looking up and down at Jackson's slacks and sports jacket. "Why? Is Carl in trouble?"

"He's dead." Jackson paused to see if anyone reacted strongly.

The woman made a pouty face. "That's a shame. He seemed nice. Lonely, but, you know, a decent guy."

The bartender gave her a look and a slight shake of his head. Jackson shifted to block her sight of him, then lightly touched her arm. "What's your name?"

"Glenda Stuck." She laughed. "I've been *stuck* with that since my marriage."

"Glenda, I'm sorry, but Carl was murdered. I'm seeking justice for him and need to contact his family."

"That's sad." Another drunk pouty face. "But I don't know anything, really. He was just someone I chatted with in here sometimes."

Behind him, the bartender said, "He mentioned a brother once, but not his name."

Jackson pivoted. "I would appreciate whatever you can tell me." Still, the guy's shifty attitude made Jackson skeptical about anything he might say.

"That's all I know. Besides that Carl drank tap beer and never tipped me."

"Did he hang out with anyone in here? A close friend?"

"No." The bartender said it too quickly.

Jackson knew he was lying. "What's your name?" He took out his notepad, hoping to make the guy uncomfortable.

"Stan Hudson. Why do you want to know?"

"Just being thorough." Jackson paused for effect. "So I can look for your name when I run a search." He met Hudson's eyes. "I really need to find his family. Tell me who Carl hung out with."

A long pause. Finally he said, "A guy named Chase, about the same age. I saw them playing pool together a few times. That's it."

"Is Chase here now?" Jackson glanced around.

"No." The bartender folded his arms across his chest. "You can't harass my customers. You're already making people uncomfortable."

"I'm trying to solve a murder. If nobody in here killed him, they should be happy to help out." Jackson cocked his head with a *wouldn't-you-agree* expression. The bartender didn't argue, so Jackson pressed. "Will you call Chase and tell him to come down here?"

"We're not that close."

"Tell me Chase's last name."

"Cortez."

It sounded like a stage name for a male stripper, but Jackson wrote it down anyway. The woman on the barstool grabbed his arm and leaned in to whisper, "I think Chase is a pimp." Her breath was hot and boozy.

"Why's that?"

"Street girls come in here looking all skanky and head straight for him. They talk for a minute, then leave." She shrugged. "Seems obvious."

Several homicide scenarios flashed in Jackson's mind. All involved drug deals or other criminal arrangements that didn't go as planned. Jackson texted Evans: *Background on Chase Cortez and Stan Hudson. ASAP.*

If the bartender was connected to Cortez, he needed to know now, before he left the tavern. Jackson looked at the drunk woman, who watched him intently. "Could the street girls be buying drugs?"

"I'm sure that's part of it."

The bartender cut in again. "Not a chance. I don't allow that shit in here."

Jackson ignored him. If Cortez was connected to Carl, their victim might show up as a *known associate*. He texted Evans again: *Look for "Carl" in Cortez file.*

Glenda set down her drink and started to slide off the stool.

Jackson lightly touched her arm. "Can I ask a few more questions?"

"Make it fast. I have to pee."

At least she wasn't intending to drive somewhere. "What did you and Carl talk about?"

"I don't remember. But I'm sure it was just casual stuff, like how hot it was this summer."

"Anything personal about him? Like a girlfriend or a hobby?"

She shook her head. "We talked baseball once, but otherwise, it's a blur."

Yeah, alcohol did that. Jackson nodded. "Thanks for your time." He handed her a business card. "If you think of anything else, call me." He turned back to the bartender, intending to do the same, but his phone beeped. A text from Evans: *Cortez has drug and theft convictions and connections to prostitutes. No Carl, but Stan Hudson is C's uncle.*

No surprise. Jackson locked eyes on the bartender.

"Chase Cortez is your nephew. You can either come to the department and explain why you lied or tell me where I can find Mr. Cortez."

The bartender's jaw tightened. "He's my sister's kid, and I only see him when he comes in here."

"Where does Chase live?"

"Over on Bell Street. I don't know the address cuz I've never been there." Hudson's tone held an undercurrent of anger.

Not with Jackson, but with his nephew. They were family, so the man was conflicted. Jackson would press for whatever information he could extract. "What does he drive?"

"A piece-of-shit red Buick Skylark." He rolled his eyes, then poured a beer for a customer who'd walked up but hadn't interrupted.

Jackson needed one more piece of information. "What does Chase look like?"

The bartender held back for a full count of three. "Kind of like me, but shorter. With a pockmarked face from all the drug lesions." Disgust seeped through, and Hudson gave in to it. "He might be right outside."

Chapter 11

Jackson scanned the dark parking lot, not seeing the car. He could barely remember the make, which had come out two decades ago and had been widely denounced as ugly. The vehicles along the front were all either compact or oversized. He walked around to the backside of the building.

There it was, parked next to a dumpster. Seemed appropriate for a pimp. The color wasn't obvious in the minimal lighting, but the style was boxy and old-school, as he'd thought. He started toward the car, subconsciously touching the weapon under his jacket. Two people sat close on the front seat, but he couldn't see them clearly.

A confrontation scene played out in his mind. Jackson stopped, pulled his phone, and called Evans.

"What's up?"

"I'm bringing in an associate of our victim. Chase Cortez. Are you still in the department?"

"Of course. Where are you?"

"The Lucky Clover on Four Corners."

"I'll be there in six minutes." Her voice tight with concern, she clicked off before he could argue.

Jackson got back into his own car and booted-up the department's database on a computer tablet he kept with him. While it loaded, he pulled his binoculars from under the seat and watched the Buick.

The man fit the vague description he'd been given, but in the dark Jackson couldn't be certain, especially since the driver wore a dark hoodie like every other thug in the country. The passenger next to him was obviously a woman. Smaller, blonde, and wearing a tank-top that sparkled.

Jackson glanced at the computer screen. The software had loaded, so he quickly keyed in the man's name. His criminal file appeared a second later. Before scanning it, Jackson looked up at the suspect's car without picking up his binoculars. The two people were still there. He skimmed through the arrest reports: possession, assault, and theft. *A real winner.*

Jackson picked up the field glasses and zeroed in on the parked couple. They seemed to be arguing. Abruptly, Cortez grabbed a handful of the woman's hair and pulled her face into his lap.

Oh crap! Jackson jumped out and jogged toward the Buick. The woman could be a prostitute and might not appreciate his interference. *Too bad.* Cortez needed a reminder that his behavior was deplorable.

Resisting the urge to pull his weapon, Jackson rapped on the windshield. Head back and eyes closed, Cortez hadn't even heard him approach. But he looked up now and jerked at the sound.

"What the fuck!" The pimp scrambled like a man caught with his pants down.

"Get out of the car with your hands up!" Jackson pulled his jacket back to show his badge and weapon. "Eugene Police. No sudden moves!"

Despite his warning, the woman grabbed a big purse from the floor of the car and bolted, running toward a vacant lot nearby. Jackson kept his eyes on Cortez.

The man climbed out, cursing. "Can I put my hands down and zip my pants?" He'd managed to button the top of his jeans in the car, but a flap of his briefs stuck out of his zipper.

"No! Turn around and put your hands on the car." Jackson didn't trust him, and a little humiliation was just what this asshole needed.

Twenty minutes later, he led Cortez into a closet-sized interrogation room and gestured for him to sit on the far side of the table. The pimp had vacillated between whining and swearing in the backseat all the way to the department, and Jackson's loathing had steadily increased.

"I'll be back with some water in a moment." He stepped sideways toward the door, keeping an eye on the pimp. Cortez was smaller than him but muscular and tense, a man ready to spring. He even wore his sandy hair combed straight back, like an old-school gangster.

"You have to take these cuffs off!" Cortez tried to sound commanding, but it came off as pleading.

"When I get back."

Jackson hurried to the break room, where he found Evans searching the fridge. She'd arrived at the tavern in time to help him get the suspect into the back of his sedan but had excused herself when they entered the department. She looked over and grinned. "I haven't had dinner."

"Me neither." His stomach growled at the thought.

"Maybe we should order something and let Cortez sit and worry while we eat."

Jackson loved the idea but rejected it. Alone time with Evans had to be limited. He didn't trust his emotions right now—or ever—around her. "No, let's get this over with."

She scowled and grabbed an apple from the fridge. "I guess this will have to hold me."

Jackson filled two paper cups with water and headed back downstairs. Evans followed, munching loudly. "I read through his file," she said with a mouthful. "Three possessions, one theft conviction, and two assault charges, both against known prostitutes. One was dropped, but he did five months for the second."

"I know. He's a pimp."

"I hate those fuckers!" She spat it out.

Her vehemence surprised him. "Me too. That's why we don't work sex crimes."

At the door, they paused. "Do we have any leverage?" Evans asked.

"No. Except that a guy he knows was shot and dumped."

"Cortez doesn't have any registered guns."

Jackson laughed. "He also doesn't have a valid driver's license."

Downstairs at the locked room, Evans waved her ID badge in front of the security unit, then held open the door. With his hands full of water, Jackson stepped inside.

"How am I supposed to drink that?" Cortez whined.

Jackson walked behind the suspect's chair and uncuffed him. "I'll leave these off for now and see how well you cooperate."

"What's this about? A blowjob in a parking lot? I could sue you for harassment."

A lot of bluster. Jackson stayed silent for a minute, hoping to make the pimp nervous. "Where were you Tuesday evening between seven and nine?"

"Why? What are you trying to blame on me?"

"Answer the question or you'll be here all night."

Cortez let out a frustrated breath. He'd been detained enough times to know the drill. "Uh, home, I think. Yeah, that's right."

"Can anyone corroborate that?" Jackson had a notepad in hand.

"Uh, my buddy Sean was hanging out."

A witness that would never materialize. "Give me Sean's last name. Carl's too."

"Carl? From the Lucky Clover?" Cortez had an edge of panic in his voice. "What's this about?"

Time to hit him hard. "Why did you kill Carl?"

Cortez blinked, snapped his mouth open and closed, then finally said, "What the hell you talkin' about?"

The suspect was either surprised or stalling. Jackson was done giving him time. "You and Carl obviously had a falling out, and he ended up dead. Care to explain?"

"What the fuck?" Cortez scooted his chair back, as though he intended to bolt. "I don't know anything about this."

"A drug deal gone bad?" Evans asked. "Or did you fight over a hooker you both laid claim to?" She managed to keep her tone light. "You really should tell us your side of it before we hear it from someone else."

"I don't have a side in this." Spit pooled in the corners of his mouth. "I swear."

"Let's start with Carl's last name," Jackson prodded. The information was still a priority.

"I don't know it. He's just someone I play pool with at the Clover."

"That's not what we hear," Jackson said.

"Who told you I know Carl? That drunk bitch who's always at the bar?" The pimp's eyes flashed with hatred. "She's a troublemaker who doesn't even know me!"

Jackson decided to back off for the moment and focus on learning more about the dead man. "Tell us what you know about Carl."

"Nothing. Except that he's a decent pool player and drinks cheap beer."

"We need his last name."

"I don't know it!"

"Where does he work? Any idea?"

"No. He didn't talk all that much."

"How long have you known him?"

Cortez rubbed his eyes. "I think he started coming into the Clover last spring, maybe April."

So their victim was a local. Or at least he hung out in Eugene intermittently. Yet so far, not a single citizen had called to identify him. The man was a shadow. Jackson remembered the pathologist's comment about the tropics. "Did Carl talk about any hobbies or places he'd been?"

Cortez paused to think about it. "You know, I think he mentioned Costa Rica once. Or maybe it was Panama. Some South American country."

Those were actually Central American locations, but Jackson didn't correct him. He needed to know more. "In what context?"

"What does that mean?" The pimp scowled.

Evans leaned in and spoke slowly. "What else were you talking about at the time?"

Cortez shrugged. "The weather?"

Jackson tried a new line of inquiry. "Did Carl ever mention a girlfriend?"

"No. I think he was afraid to talk to women, like they were too good for him." Cortez scoffed. "As if!"

Evans tensed beside him, so Jackson quickly asked, "Who

else at the tavern knew Carl?"

"Nobody really. He was kind of a loner. I only knew him because we played pool."

This was getting nowhere. But Jackson had one last line of questioning. "Do you drive another vehicle besides the Skylark?"

"Uh, that's my girlfriend's car."

Jackson had the plate number, so ownership would be easy to check out. "We know you don't have a license, but we still want to know about your vehicle."

Cortez slumped and was silent for a while. "I own a Ford pickup, but it just sits in the driveway."

A truck! Jackson felt his first glimmer of hope.

Chapter 12

Thursday, September 19, 6:45 a.m.

Dallas dug through her luggage for running shoes. Her hotel suite had a bedroom and dresser, but she hadn't bothered to unpack everything yet. The fact that the bureau had approved a hotel room rather than a furnished apartment meant that her boss didn't expect the assignment to take more than a week or two. She wished it represented confidence in her skills, but she guessed the decision was more about cost efficiency and pressure to get the job done. The space was decent for a mid-level hotel and even had a view of a nearby park. Still, the lighting was bad and the carpet smelled funny.

She felt the pressure too. A predator was escalating—and women's lives were at stake. She would work around-the-clock until they nailed him.

After another quick look at the assault-scene map, Dallas tucked her key card and phone into a narrow waist pack and headed out. She intended to jog around the university and check out the bars in the area where the victims had been assaulted. Her body wanted a workout, and her brain needed to visualize the locations, so she was multitasking—and loved it. The excursion could take hours, and she hoped to find water somewhere along the way.

As she ran down a side street, the crisp cool air and lovely green trees gave her a quiet sense of joy. Back home, Phoenix sucked as a place to exercise outside. The air was too damn hot and stagnant, and the scenery was nothing but boring buildings and scraggly cacti. So this moment felt glorious. When she reached the campus, with its large grassy spaces, the aesthetics were even better. In places, she could see Mt. Hood in the distance, a spectacular view. Maybe she should put in for a transfer.

And leave Cameron?

Dallas smiled. She felt this way with almost every new place she visited. But clearly, she needed to spend more weekends in Flagstaff, which wasn't quite as lovely as this area but still greener and more mountainous than downtown Phoenix. For years, she'd avoided Flagstaff because she'd grown up there and the memories were mostly negative. With Cameron in the picture, that was changing.

Her plan was to cross the campus, check out the bars on the other side, then circle back around the perimeter to cover the rest of the assault locations. She jogged down a wide path that eventually opened into a large circular area adorned with rectangular concrete blocks that resembled a strange mini-Stonehenge. Not her idea of art, but not the worst effort she'd seen either.

On the other side of the plaza, she ran toward a narrow path between two oversized buildings. Constructed of concrete, wood, and glass, the odd rustic-modern mix seemed to work. Dallas slowed her pace, watching for intersecting sidewalks and students who might suddenly step out of side doors or from behind trees. It was early, so she hadn't seen many young people yet, but the few she'd encountered had been staring at their phones. Accidents waiting to happen.

A bearded guy stepped into her path about ten feet away. Hearing her footsteps, he pivoted, then grinned. Dallas steered to the left to go around him. As she passed, he reached out, grabbed her ponytail, and jerked her toward him. "Hey, blondie. Where are you—"

The scalp pain and abruptness triggered her training. Instinctively, she stepped into the pull, knocking him off balance. Dallas reached back with her left hand and gouged a thumb deep into the tender part of his wrist, forcing him to loosen his grip on her hair. At the same time, she threw a twisting upward punch with her other hand. The flat of her knuckles hit him square in his windpipe. The man made a strange gasping noise and his eyes went wide.

He tried to speak, but couldn't. Still on autopilot, Dallas landed a kick to his groin, and the jerk collapsed to his knees. Her impulse was to kick him in the nose too, but she forced herself to back off. She didn't want to deal with police officers or blow her cover. With her cell phone, she snapped a picture of his face, then jogged away.

Stupid troglodyte. She would send the image to her local FBI contact and let them track down the man's identity—just in case he turned out to be the rapist. But that seemed unlikely. Their suspect had a pattern—drug a woman's drink, then assault her when she passed out. That bearded guy was just an asshole opportunist. She glanced back and saw him still on the ground. For a second, she almost felt sorry for him. He'd stupidly grabbed the wrong "blondie." Maybe he wouldn't make that mistake again.

She wished high schools would teach self-defense to all young women. Growing up with drug- and alcohol-addicted parents had taught her to fend for herself at an early age. Her dad's jackass friends had tried grabbing a feel of her budding breasts or sticking their hands down her pants. Fortunately, she'd been born with a certain fearlessness. By grade school, she'd learned to bite hard and run fast.

In high school, she'd not only taken acting classes, she'd also learned martial arts from a teacher who had a crush on her. The combination had crystalized her self-confidence into a fortitude that allowed her to step outside herself and take on protective personalities. She called it *survival mode.* The only time she didn't feel that way at all was when she was with Cameron.

The thought almost brought her to a stop. Maybe it *was* time to break off with him. She'd never wanted to be that attached to anyone. But she couldn't think about that now. She'd reached the edge of the campus. Time to start scouting out the bars where women had been assaulted. Across the street stood Tyler's Bar & Grill, a white-brick building where the first assault had taken place. The woman had woken in a back hall—when an employee found her and tried to kick her out, thinking she was drunk. The victim's memory of the overall attack was vague, but she was certain a man had stuck his fingers into her vagina.

Dallas jogged around to the rear of the bar, putting herself into the mind of the suspect. Why the back hall? Did he work here? Or had he just assaulted the woman in the first private place he came to? More important, would he circle back to this tavern for his next victim? So far, the perp had shifted to a new location with each attack, except the last time. So she thought he might be cycling through the campus drinking holes again. Still, the big question remained. Was he a student, or did he just find college girls to be easy victims? Dallas had her money on the latter.

As she cruised through the back lot, she noted the location of the rear door, the nearby dumpster, and a stack of flattened cardboard. She rounded the building, got on the sidewalk, and ran east. Students were suddenly everywhere. The first class of the morning must have let out. She picked up her pace, hoping to blend in, despite being ten years older than the average freshman. But her age wasn't important. When she went out on her first bait mission, all that would matter was her looks—and vulnerability.

At noon, she sauntered into a hole-in-the-wall cafe a few blocks from her hotel and sat at a small table in the back, as instructed. An old guy in a lavender apron came over and handed her a laminated menu. Dallas ordered coffee, hoping to warm up. In Phoenix, it was still hot as hell—but not here. She'd been cold since her run.

As she sipped her black coffee, the tiny place filled up. Halfway through her cup, a woman in workout clothes approached. "Can I share your table?"

Her local contact. Dallas nodded. "Sure."

The woman sat down, and Dallas looked her over. Forty-five, short dark hair, a pleasant-but-not-quite-pretty face, and a rock-solid body. The undercover agent wasn't who she'd expected, but Dallas was pleased they'd sent a woman. Especially considering the nature of her assignment. "I'm Amber, by the way."

"Jan Keller." The agent reached for the plastic menu. "What do you recommend?"

"Not the coffee." Dallas laughed and pushed hers aside.

The aging waiter walked up. "What can I get for you ladies?"

Dallas ordered a small bowl of chili. Agent Keller's brow

tightened in the slightest way. "I'll have a cup of vegetable soup."

"Either of you want cornbread?" the waiter asked.

"No, thanks," they said in unison.

The old guy shrugged and walked away.

They sat quietly, reading on their phones, supposed strangers. The food arrived a few minutes later, and Dallas dug right into her chili, wishing she'd ordered a larger size. After a few bites, she looked up. "I heard that Tyler's Bar & Grill on campus has a great menu. Have you eaten there?"

Keller, if that was even her real name, shook her head. "No, but I've listened to a few local bands play, and they serve wine. So the place is okay."

"I'll check it out tonight." Dallas kept her voice casual, but the meaning would be clear.

Keller's expression changed for the first time. A small smile. She quickly finished her soup and picked up her check, sliding her hand across the table as she did. Dallas reached out and pulled the tiny flat package into her fingers. Probably the GPS tracker the bureau wanted her to wear.

"Have a nice day." Keller got up and walked toward the cashier.

Dallas watched her intently, memorizing the agent's size, shape, and gait. She might look completely different tonight when she showed up at Tyler's. But Dallas wouldn't. Keller's job would be to keep an eye on her, no matter which bar she staked out. Now that they'd met, Dallas would keep Keller posted by text. With any luck, they'd bust the guy quickly. Maybe a few of his online friends too.

Chapter 13

Thursday, 7:05 a.m.

After another short night of sleep, Jackson backed out of the driveway and tried to get psyched up for another long workday. He decided to skip checking in at the department and get straight into the field. His first stop would be within a mile of the Lucky Clover where he'd picked up their suspect the night before. He'd booked Chase Cortez into jail on *indecent exposure* charges, hoping the county lockup would keep him until an arraignment this morning. If the hunch he intended to check out paid off, Jackson would get a search warrant and maybe arrest Cortez again. He knew right where to find him.

The house on the corner sported a new roof, but the paint was faded and the landscaping overgrown. The mix suggested that the owner was a landlord who protected their investment but didn't care much about the property beyond that.

The red Buick Skylark from the Lucky Clover sat in the driveway—but no truck. Unless it was in the attached narrow garage or parked by the house on the other side. Jackson drove around the corner and saw a blue Ford F150 on a gravel pad. He parked and hustled over to the vehicle's back end. The sense that he only had a few minutes made his heart pound a little harder than he liked.

He examined the tailgate on both sides—it seemed undamaged—then took some quick pictures of the cargo's interior. A pile of rags, a beat-up gas can, and a dog leash. In a few steps, he rounded the truck bed, scanning for anything that might indicate the victim had been back there. Specifically, he hoped to spot either fresh blood or bits of black plastic. No luck with that.

A woman's voice bellowed out the side window. "Get off my property or I'm calling the cops!"

Jackson almost laughed as he hustled back to his car, but his disappointment overrode it. The effort hadn't panned out. The pickup might still be their best evidence, but he wouldn't know until they could examine it at the crime lab. That wouldn't happen until he had enough cause to file a search warrant. For the moment, Cortez was just the victim's acquaintance, who happened to own a truck. He'd hit another dead end on the case until someone else recognized Carl. He had time to honor his promise to Kera.

A few minutes later, Jackson crossed over the railroad tracks and promptly slowed. His right turn was just up ahead. The quaint neighborhood where the missing woman lived was wedged between River Road and the water itself, isolated from other housing by an undeveloped area, euphemistically called a park, and a real park that served as access to walking paths and a footbridge over to the mall.

The address Kera had given belonged to a small green house with an enclosed carport that took up most of the driveway. He guessed that the garage behind it had been converted into living space, a common home remodel now that rent was unaffordable for low-wage earners.

Jackson parked fifty yards away—not wanting to alert the occupants to his presence—and walked toward the faded front door. The lawn was brown, the flowers dried and droopy. But it was September. The rain hadn't started yet, and everyone was tired of summer watering. A lot of yards looked similar. He pushed the doorbell but didn't hear it chime. Jackson knocked loudly. No sound came from inside. He pounded again and waited, noticing the blinds on the front window were closed and the porch light was on—even though it was a bright sunny morning.

How much time should he give this effort? He'd only committed to stopping by. He wanted to help Kera's client, but he still didn't know his homicide victim's last name. That case had to remain his priority. Still, not having a full ID, combined with near-certainty that Carl was a non-resident drug dealer, gave him a little leeway to check out this missing surrogate.

Stepping back from the door, Jackson walked over to the plywood carport and glanced into the open front. A silver Toyota that looked like it had endured twenty years of abuse filled most of the space. If this was the woman's main transportation, she was probably home—or something weird had happened to her.

Jackson jogged back to the main house, knocked again, and shouted, "Eugene Police! If you're in there, please respond!"

Silence. Except for a couple of noisy birds in the backyard. He checked the door, found it locked, and shouted again, this time using Bettina's name. As he started around the house, a voice called out behind him. Jackson turned to see a woman coming up the walkway. She had pretty silver hair and a small dog on a leash.

"I heard you say 'police.' Is something wrong?" She flashed a tight smile and zipped her sweater against the cool morning air.

Jackson decided to solicit whatever help he could. "Do you know Bettina Rios, the woman who lives here?"

"Sort of. We chat briefly sometimes when we pass on the street, but I haven't seen her in a while."

"Any idea where she is?"

She shook her head. "That's why I walked over when I heard you. I'm a little worried. It's not like her to be gone. I think she even works at home."

"Maybe she took a trip to the coast with friends?" A plausible reason she might have left town without her car.

"I rarely see her with anyone, and no one comes to the house. But Bettina mentioned taking care of her mother once."

A sick feeling gripped Jackson's gut. Caregivers could get burned out, but few women ever abandoned their children or mothers. He felt himself getting sucked into the case, and he had to follow through now. "Do you know her mother's name or location?"

"Sorry."

"Do you know if Bettina kept a key somewhere accessible?"

The neighbor grimaced. "I didn't know her that well. I've only been in this area about six months." She pulled her hand out of her pocket. "I'm Karen Silas, by the way."

Jackson shook it, then handed his notepad to her. "Give me your phone number, in case I need to follow up."

As she wrote it down, she commented, "Bettina went out running every morning. I know because I take my dog out around the same time and often see her. But not this week."

Jackson took back his notepad and jotted *morning run.* "Anything else you know about her?"

"She mentioned an ex-boyfriend once but didn't elaborate."

"Tell me the last time you saw her."

"I think it was Saturday morning."

"What time?"

"Six-thirty."

Jackson made another note. Once he wrote information down, it stayed with him. "Was that her usual routine?"

"As far as I know."

"Did she ever talk about the baby or her surrogacy contract?"

"What?" Her stunned expression spoke for itself. "Bettina was pregnant?"

"Yes, but at this point, I'd better not discuss her private business." The surrogate must not have developed much of a belly yet. "Any idea where she would go if she relocated?"

Silas shook her head.

"Based on your concern, I'm going in for a welfare check."

"Please let me know what you find out."

"You can call our PR person in a few days." Jackson started to walk away, then turned back. "What does Bettina look like?" He would check out the missing woman online later, but he wanted to be able to visualize her now.

"Tiny and pretty, with dark hair and eyes. She looks Hispanic. Probably in her mid-twenties." The neighbor hesitated for a moment, then blurted, "I think she might be here illegally. That would explain why she's such a recluse."

"Thanks."

Her status didn't matter much to him. In the past, to keep his job manageable, he had often divided people into split categories. Cops and civilians. Criminals and non-criminals. Citizens and non-citizens. Over time, he'd come to realize it was never that simple. He would rather seek justice for an innocent noncitizen than for a criminal with a US birth certificate. Over the years, he'd learned that homicide victims were often less than honorable.

Jackson shifted and stared at the house, thinking about his options. He could call Sergeant Bruckner and have him bring the doorknocker. But the huge steel cylinder did a lot of damage, and he didn't know enough to justify that. Maybe she'd left a key somewhere. So many people did, often to their regret. Jackson hurried toward the back of the house, ignoring the twinges of pain from his incision. A partially open window would work too—if he wasn't too sore to make the climb.

The house was locked up tight, and he couldn't find a spare key. He sized up the back door. Old and hollow, with an ancient lock. He hadn't busted open a door in years, but what the hell. He took a step back, turned sideways, and threw his weight and shoulder into the aging wood. It cracked down the center as though he'd taken an axe to it. *Oh crap!* The latch plate had pulled loose from the frame too. He gave the door another hard hit and stumbled inside as it gave way.

Rubbing his now-painful shoulder, Jackson looked around. Nothing amiss and no sign of a struggle. Relieved, he checked the kitchen sink. Dry. He moved quickly through the small space, where a thick musty scent hung over everything. No one had opened a window recently.

The door to a bedroom stood ajar, so he stepped inside. Tidy, with a colorful bedcover. Jackson opened a few dresser drawers. All were about two-thirds full. Had Bettina packed some of her clothes? Or was this her standard inventory? The closet was stuffed though, indicating she hadn't taken much, if anything. In the adjoining bathroom, makeup sat on the counter. Women never left their beauty products willingly, so it seemed doubtful she'd left town voluntarily to keep the other woman's baby. Unless the surrogate was devious and wanted everything to look as though she'd been abducted.

He remembered what the neighbor had said, and a scene played out in his mind. Bettina had locked up, gone out for a run, and never returned. He visualized the nearby bike path along the river. Would they find her body soon? She supposedly had a mother she'd been taking care of. Why hadn't the mom called in her disappearance? Was she aware of the scheme . . . if there was one? More of what the neighbor said fell into place. If the mother was here illegally as well, maybe she was afraid to contact the police.

The stench in the bathroom was suddenly unbearable. *Where was that coming from? The sewer?* Jackson stepped into the bedroom and glanced around for a computer or phone. He didn't spot either. A quick search, including under the mattress, didn't reveal any electronics, valuables, or cash. The room was so barren, the effort only took a few minutes.

Back in the hall, a waft of decay hit him hard—followed by a queasy stomach. Only one thing smelled that way. He hurried to the living area and crossed through the kitchen. The stink intensified.

The door to what had originally been the garage had been removed, replaced with long strips of beads. Dreading what he would find, he pushed through the flexible divider. A barrage of trinkets, vases, pillows, and colorful paintings assaulted his eyes. Combined with the smell, the room overwhelmed him for a moment. He glanced to the right and saw a woman in a wheelchair—who looked quite dead.

Something scraped the floor behind him. Jackson spun toward the sound. The back part of the garage had been partitioned off, maybe for storage. Was there an animal in there? No, those were footsteps.

He rushed to the makeshift door, yanked it open, and yelled "Stop!"

On the other side of the cluttered space, the exterior door slammed shut. Jackson leaped over a lawnmower and rushed outside. Across the backyard, a man jumped onto the fence and scrambled over.

"Police! Stop!" His instinct was to chase the guy down, but he didn't want to leave the potential crime scene unattended, and he knew his chance of catching the guy was slim.

Jackson reached for his phone, taking a mental image of the man's description at the same time. He pressed 911 and identified himself. "I need patrol units in the Chambers/River Road area. Suspect is male, five-ten or so, and muscular, with light-brown hair. Wearing faded jeans, a gray sweatshirt, and bright-green tennis shoes." Jackson paused, trying to map out where the perp might run. "He may be headed for the bike path along the river, so send a unit to VRC in case he crosses the pedestrian bridge." That's what he would do if he were fleeing this area. Cross the river and disappear inside the mall for a while.

"Got it." The dispatcher spoke into another mic for a moment, then projected her voice back to him. "Is he armed?"

"I'm not sure." Jackson hurried back inside. "Let me check something while I have you on the line." He crossed through the storage area and back into the converted bedroom space.

Slumped over in her wheelchair, the old woman showed no blood or wounds he could see. But much of her chest wasn't visible. Still, she'd been dead a while. Why had the perp stayed in her house? Or was the guy just an opportunistic thief?

"You still there?" the dispatcher asked.

"Yeah. Notify Sergeant Lammers that we have a body and ask her to send my team."

"Where might that be?" A hint of teasing.

Jackson rattled off the Briarcliff address, then added, "It's a little area near Maurie Jacobs Park."

"Got it."

For a moment, he stood motionless, trying to assess the situation. A dead body, a missing woman, and a fleeing suspect. This wasn't even his case! How should he prioritize his time? He glanced at the poor woman again and noticed the phone in her lap, still partially in her hand. If the perp was just a thief, why hadn't he taken it?

Jackson pinched the corner of the phone with two fingertips, pulled it free, and slid the device into his pocket. Once he had gloves on, he would check to see who the dead lady had been trying to call.

As he hurried back to his car to get his satchel, an odd thought hit him. The man going over the fence had been the same size—and worn the same style of clothes—as Chase Cortez. *But what the hell would the pimp be doing here?*

Chapter 14

Footsteps sounded above her, and Bettina sat up, terrified. He was home again. *Please don't let him come down.* She scooted to the edge of the moldy mattress and pushed to her feet. Thinking about what he'd done to her and would do again made hot tears pool in her eyes. *No!* She wiped them away. No more crying. No more despair. He wasn't worthy of it. Rage surfaced and she embraced it. The *pendejo* who'd abducted her would not get away with this. She would find a way out—or a way to hurt him. At some point, she expected him to try to kill her. That's when she would fight with everything she had.

For now, she played along, pretending to be his girlfriend like he'd asked her to. She was working up the nerve to request real food. Fruit and protein the baby needed, instead of cold pizza and cereal. Bettina rubbed her lower belly and whispered, "Don't worry, little one. I'll keep you safe as long as I can."

How long had she been here? She thought it might be Thursday, but she wasn't sure. One morning, she'd been out running, then someone had grabbed her, and she'd woken up in this hell-hole.

The man hadn't told her his name, insisting she call him 'Sweetie.' The thought of saying it made a bitter sound burst from her throat. She'd done it a few times, just to keep him calm, but she'd almost gagged. In her mind, she changed his name to Sweaty.

Bettina took a step, and the chain between her ankles clanked against the concrete floor. *Hijo de puta!* The damn noise bothered her almost as much as the restriction. Maybe she could convince him to remove the shackles. The freak actually thought she might start to like him. As bizarre as that seemed, his need for affection made him somewhat malleable.

Bettina listened for more movement upstairs. The house was quiet, except for the muted sound of a TV that was always on. She shuffled around the perimeter of the concrete room, rubbing her abdomen and humming a bedtime song her mother had sung to her as a child. Poor Mama! When Bettina felt calmer, she ran her hands along the cool, damp walls. She'd already done it a dozen times—and searched every inch of the room. It was a concrete box. Except for the weird door at the top of the stairs. She'd clanked up there once when he seemed to be gone, but the metal plate and steel locks were impenetrable.

The only vulnerability in the dark space was the narrow horizontal window at the top of the wall opposite the stairs. A dirty film covered the glass on the outside, letting in just enough light that she could see to function, but it obscured anyone from seeing inside.

None of that mattered because she couldn't reach it. Not even by standing on the metal pot in the corner, which she'd tried. The only other items in the room were the mattress and a stained loveseat with no backrest or foot braces. Sometimes he made her sit on the ugly thing with him and "talk, like a real couple would." She'd also tried to drag the seat over to the window, but it was heavy so the task had been slow and loud. He'd heard the commotion and put a stop to any further effort by removing the foot pegs.

And punished her for trying.

Bettina shuddered. How long could she live like this? Women around the world had been held captive for years, even decades. Some had even given birth to their abductor's children. She'd left her home country to avoid being taken by a drug lord, and what good had that done? Bettina hugged herself. What would this man do when her belly got big and he realized she was pregnant?

Poor Erica. Her client probably thought she'd disappeared with her baby. Had Erica called the police? Had anyone checked on Mama? Bettina couldn't let herself think about her poor mother, sitting alone, calling and calling, trying to reach her, wondering why she'd been abandoned. But the stubborn old woman wouldn't ask anyone for help or call the police. She'd always been afraid of them—in both countries—but now with her dementia, Mama was afraid of everyone but her daughter.

The pressure on Bettina's bladder reached a breaking point. She trudged over to the bucket toilet and relieved herself. Sweaty had promised to put in a real bathroom someday "if things went well." *Whatever the hell that meant.* Another harsh scoff erupted from her throat. The *pendejo* actually thought he could win her over by telling her she was pretty and sharing stories about his childhood.

Which had been a nightmare . . . if she could believe him. But none of it mattered. She was his prisoner and sex slave, and she would kill him to escape if she ever got the opportunity. She prayed that moment was coming. The last time he'd been down, she'd begged him for warm water and soap to bathe herself, and he'd promised to bring her a bucket soon.

Bettina imagined him coming through the trapdoor with a heavy bucket. For a moment—before he set down the water and locked the entry behind him—he would be vulnerable. And the door would be open. What if she got into position at the top of the stairs, ready and waiting? Could she knock him off balance and run out? Not a chance. He was too solid. She needed a weapon. A nice fat baseball bat to smash against his head.

She also needed her shackles removed.

The stairs rose up in front of her, taunting her with an escape route that led nowhere. Wooden, rickety stairs that creaked loudly when the man stepped on them, sending shivers down her spine.

Wood! That could be a weapon. Could she break off a piece of step and use it to club him? Bettina looked at her small weak hands and sighed. She would try anyway.

After making her fingers bleed, she finally gave up. She clasped the painful abrasions together and tried to pray. But her conversation with God quickly turned into an accusation. *Why?* After everything she'd already been through? Raped at the age of thirteen by a gang member proving himself as part of his initiation. A second MS thug had watched and laughed. *Where were you then, God?* Bettina cried again, this time with rage.

The journey to America had taken so long and been so difficult. Memories flooded her. Sleeping on the ground and begging for food. Watching her mother age a little every day. Walking, worrying, and grieving for her younger brother Javier, who'd been beheaded just for challenging the drug dealers in their area. Six long treacherous weeks on the road, her feet so battered they would never be the same, and they'd finally made it.

Now this.

Why, dear God? Bettina didn't understand.

Footsteps sounded near the top of the stairs. He was coming.

Bettina braced herself for another sexual assault. But he surprised her by sitting on the little couch and patting the seat beside him. "Come, sit by me. Have a sandwich."

She could barely stand to look at him, but she would go along. Whatever it took to stay alive—and not get too badly hurt in the process.

He stretched his arm and held out the food bribe. Starving, Bettina grabbed the sandwich and took a bite, ignoring her dislike of ham and fake cheese. Suddenly self-conscious about her rounded little belly, she scooted over and sat down. He squeezed her leg. "I really want you to like me," he said. "Like a girlfriend would. What can I do?"

Bettina choked on her food. "That's—" She caught herself and tried again. "This is a very unusual"—she paused, searching for the right word—"situation. Maybe you should start by bringing me some fruit or vegetables. I'll get scurvy down here if I don't eat right."

"What's scurvy?"

It surprised her that he didn't know. "A disease caused by lack of vitamins."

"I'll just buy you a jar of vitamins."

She decided to push back. "I thought you wanted me to like you."

He scratched his dirty hair. "Okay. I'll get some bananas. What else would make you attracted to me? I mean, if we were on a date."

A small spark of pity. Did he really believe he could still

win her over? How delusional and sad. *Yet,* she reminded herself, *he was a sociopath and didn't see her as a person.* She could never forget that. She had to force herself to get through this. "If we went out to dinner, for example, you would ask me about myself. That would make me think you cared about me and lead me to like you in return." Her words were so careful, she hardly recognized her own voice.

He thought it over for a moment. "What kind of music do you like?"

"Anything with a rhythmic beat." Would he actually bring her a radio or something?

"I'll think about it." He squeezed her leg again. "Where were you born?"

"Does it matter?" Being defensive about her status was pointless now. "Guatemala. I came here with my mother last year." *For the second time.*

"You know what's funny? My mother moved from here to—" He stopped and tensed. "Never mind. I guess everyone wants to be somewhere else." He grabbed at her clothes. "Take off your pants."

Her jaw clamped down. She couldn't stop him, but she might be able to make it more bearable. "Another way to make me like you is for you to be considerate of me."

"How?"

"Besides the fruit, bring me a sweater. And take off these shackles, so I can walk normal."

He didn't respond.

She hated herself for what she was about to say, but she had to anyway. "And please use lubricant so it's not so painful for me."

His brow furrowed. "Is sex always painful for women?"

He was so strangely naive. "Only when they're raped."

"I don't understand how it's different."

Was he mentally handicapped or just uneducated? He seemed to have no social aptitude. But she might as well keep stalling. "If a woman is excited and into sex, she secretes fluid in her vagina to lubricate it. But most of us are only into sex if we like or love the guy."

He was quiet for a long moment. "I'll go get some lube."

Chapter 15

Thursday, 5:05 p.m.

At his desk, Jackson ordered deli meals for five people, then opened a Word doc for his case notes. Forcing himself to focus on the gunshot homicide, he typed up the circumstances surrounding the discovery of the body and added what he knew from the autopsy. Beyond that, all he had was a first name and a known associate. Even if Carl was a drug mule or criminal of some type, he still deserved justice, or at least closure, Jackson reminded himself. More important, the person who killed him needed to be locked up and off the streets.

Yet he couldn't stop thinking about Bettina Rios and her poor mother. After examining the old woman's body at the death scene, the medical examiner had suggested that Serena Rios had likely died of a stroke or heart attack. Natural causes. He would know more after the autopsy. *If* Lammers let him work the Rios case. Jackson took a deep breath and called her.

His boss picked up on the third ring and snapped, "You've already ruined my day. What now?"

Ruined it by reporting a death and a disappearance? Her annoyance was so strange he ignored it. "I have a task force meeting scheduled, and I thought you might like to attend."

A long pause. "I guess I'd better if I want to stay informed."

An indirect complaint that he didn't update her often enough. He let that go too. Now that he knew she had chronic pain, he cut her more slack. "The meeting starts in twenty minutes."

"Nice heads up."

The line went dead. Jackson used his desk phone to call Zapata, the only detective assigned to handle missing-person cases. The poor guy was so overworked he probably wouldn't answer. Jackson left him a message about Bettina and invited him to attend the meeting as well. Since nobody had actually filed a report yet, Jackson hoped to keep the case and let his team work it. His gut told him Bettina's disappearance would end up with his unit anyway.

He opened a second Word doc and summarized everything he knew about the missing woman, including what he'd learned from her mother's phone and their shared house. Jackson transferred the files to a server that his team could access as they gathered more information.

After printing multiple copies of both files—a habit he couldn't break—he gathered all his paperwork and headed into the conference room across the wide hall.

As usual, Evans was already seated and reading her own notes. She looked up and gave him a worried smile. "I don't know what you plan to talk about, cuz we've got nothing."

The team had spent part of the afternoon searching Bettina Rios' home and come up mostly empty-handed. But Evans probably meant their mystery man case. "Any new leads on Carl?"

Evans shook her head. "I talked to six homeowners along Crow Road yesterday, and nobody recognized him."

Rob Schakowski hustled into the room, looking leaner

than his barrel-shaped body ever had. His buzz-cut hair was completely gray now, and the weight loss made his face sag.

Still, Evans whistled in appreciation. "What's your secret? I know you didn't give up pizza."

"I've been doing Zumba workouts with the wife." He grinned and shrugged. "It's weird but still better than dieting . . . or learning to live alone."

Evans burst into laughter. "I'd give anything to watch you dance."

He sat across from her. "Never gonna happen." Schak pivoted to Jackson. "Are we taking this missing-person case or what? We didn't find a damn thing of interest in that house."

"Except Bettina's phony driver's license," Evans reminded him.

"We don't know their status yet." As Jackson spoke, Lammers strode in.

Six-feet tall and built like a meat locker, she commanded attention even before she boomed orders. "Let's make this quick. I'd like to get home before our dinner guests arrive."

Evans stood and walked to the whiteboard. She wrote *Carl* across the top and added *Known Associate*s underneath. Below that, she listed *Chase Cortez* and *Lucky Clover tavern.* She turned back to the group. "Remind me of the autopsy details." Evans seemed a little off her game, but she'd probably slept even less than he had.

"Purple scars from infected bug bites and a heart tattoo on his chest." Jackson paused to let her catch up. "And time spent in Costa Rica or some other Central American country."

"I showed his image to tattoo shops," Schak added. "But nobody recognized him. They also said heart tattoos are too common to have any kind of artistic signature."

While Evans added the information to the board, Jackson passed out his case notes. "The fact that no one has identified him makes me think he hasn't been in the area long."

"Maybe he's just a private person," Lammers suggested.

"Or a drug mule." Jackson glanced down at the complete autopsy report that had come in that afternoon. "The pathologist found needle marks between his toes and blood clots consistent with long-term heroin use."

"Good thing we're spending all this time trying to find his killer," Schak muttered.

They'd all had similar frustrations, but nobody ever voiced them. Lammers gave Schak a look. "Do you want off this case? Off this team?"

"No, ma'am." Schak looked chagrinned. "Sorry I said that."

Jackson wanted to move along. "I sent Carl's photo to the bureau, but they don't have any record of him either."

"Hold a press conference," Lammers instructed. "If you ask the public directly, you'll get a better response."

Jackson cringed but tried to hide it. "If we don't get an ID soon, I will."

Someone rapped on the door, then pushed it open. Jackson waved in the desk officer carrying a big sack. She set it on the table. "Bon appétit."

Jackson dumped out a jumble of sandwiches, cookies, and small bags of chips. Schak made a face, but grabbed his share. A moment later, Evans absentmindedly did too as she read through the second page of notes.

Lammers helped herself to a chocolate chip cookie. "As I mentioned, I have dinner guests this evening, so let's keep this moving."

"There's more here you didn't tell us." Evans looked up from reading. "The victim had moss on his boots, indicating he hung out around water. And chewing tobacco in his pocket." She went back to the board.

"Any response to that?" Jackson asked.

"He's rural," Schak offered. "Or maybe he works at the Fern Ridge marina."

"Good thought. Why don't you check it out?"

Lammers stared at the board. "Who's Chase Cortez? How is he connected?

"He's a pimp who sometimes played pool with our victim." Jackson could hear his own frustration. "We interrogated him but got nowhere. He claims he doesn't even know Carl's last name."

"Doesn't mean he didn't shoot him," Schak muttered. "Does he have an alibi?"

Jackson realized he hadn't checked it out. He was off his game too. "Not really. Cortez claims he was with a friend, but doesn't know his last name either."

"Millennials," Evans said, rolling her eyes.

They all laughed, even Lammers. Jackson reached for his second set of notes and passed them around.

"What's this?" The sergeant shook the paper, her good humor gone. "Are you assuming charge of the Rios case just because you stumbled onto it?" She tipped her head and looked over her new glasses. "What led you to check on the missing woman in the first place?"

Jackson hated to involve Kera, but the surrogate contract could be a factor in Bettina's disappearance. "My girlfriend, who works at a fertility clinic, said one of her patients was concerned that her surrogate had disappeared." Jackson paused, knowing it was a lot to process.

"Oh for fuck's sake." Lammers stared at him. "The missing woman is pregnant with someone else's baby? And they had an official contract?"

"Correct. The biological mother got worried when she couldn't reach Bettina."

Lammers seemed mildly amused now. "Maybe she disappeared on purpose so she could keep the baby. Wouldn't be the first time."

Jackson shook his head. "Considering that Bettina cared for her disabled mother—who died in her absence—that seems unlikely." He picked up Selena Rios' phone from the table. "She called her daughter seven times between Saturday and Tuesday when she died. Bettina never picked up."

A moment of silence.

Evans tapped her copy of the case notes. "We just need to find her ex. It's always the abusive boyfriend." She opened her tablet and quickly got online. "I'm checking Facebook for a connection."

As Evans searched, Jackson updated Lammers on his strange afternoon. "Someone was in the converted garage area when I checked the house. The intruder ran out the back and leapt over the fence. Five-ten with light-brown hair. He's stocky, one-ninety or so. Faded jeans, gray sweatshirt, and bright-green tennis shoes. I have officers statewide looking for him."

Evans glanced up. "That sounds like Chase Cortez."

"I know. That's another reason I want to keep this second case."

"You said Carl was a drug mule?" Schak rubbed his head. "Cortez probably knows him better than he admits."

"I think so too. Maybe we need to talk to one of Cortez's girls."

"I'm on it," Evans said.

"So you think Cortez might have been in the missing woman's house?" Lammers sounded as skeptical as she'd ever been. "But why? What could possibly be the connection?"

Jackson hadn't had time to formulate a theory and felt his cheeks flush.

"What if Bettina's a mule too?" Schak asked. "Maybe they were both bringing narcotics from Central America."

"Possibly. I ran her name in the database and nothing came up. But I haven't done facial recognition on her yet." Jackson suddenly felt overwhelmed with both cases. They needed Detective Quince on the team, but he was out of town on his own investigation.

Evans cleared her throat. "I just found Bettina's photo on a Facebook page. That guy you saw? It probably wasn't Cortez." She shifted her tablet around so they could see the image. "This is Aaron Russo, her ex-boyfriend. He fits your description perfectly."

Chapter 16

Thursday, 5:35 p.m.

Dallas opened a beer and sat on the hotel couch with her work laptop. The bureau always issued PCs, and she'd never liked the operating system. Macs were more user-friendly, but for this job it didn't matter.

She logged into her new Facebook page as Amber Davison and checked for friend requests: *67!* Blonde hair, boobs, and a pretty face were popular assets. Some days she hated her looks and wished she'd been born almost anything else. Most undercover work required blending in, so for her, that meant wigs or dye, sunglasses, and chest wraps. Because most criminals were men, the bureau took full advantage of her attractiveness and sent her into situations where she could exploit male vulnerability—like this one.

She accepted all the requests, scanning each profile for a Vancouver location. Three of the guys who friended her were local. She sent brief messages to each, then doubled back to check out their links and Twitter profiles. None were posting openly as *TribalDragon, JungleBoy*, or any other personas she'd seen in the incel forum. Time to set the bait anyway. Keeping it simple, she updated her FB status: *Dancing at Tyler's tonight! #girlsjustwannahavefun #gonnabewild*

She repeated the post on Instagram, then switched

browsers and logged into the Not Normal site as *bi*chgirlhater*. Scrolling down, she found a thread called *Where the Cunts Are*. Disgusting, but the appropriate conversation for what she needed. Dallas read through a few comments, found a reference to schools, then keyed in a post she hoped would generate a response: *My dead town doesnt have college so the bar scene is pathetic. Nuthin but dicks n old pussy.*

She'd posted on the site several times the day before and felt ready to push the subject. This gig wasn't a long-term operation to stop a network of nonviolent fraud. It had to be quick and dirty. Women's lives were at stake, and every day mattered. If the suspect followed his escalating pattern, he was due to strike again.

TribalDragon quickly posted back: *Florida is da bomb. Lots of T&A everywere even if u dont get laid.*

Shuddering at the lack of spelling and grammar—which she had to imitate to fit in—Dallas typed: *I'll chek it out. Where do u hang to hook up with easy fems?*

The online conversation got quiet for a minute, so she went to the fridge for another beer. When she returned, she took a moment to check out the interior links to other incel sites. And found whole new groups of men with bizarre profile names and forums where they posted about being bullied as children and about hating their own looks.

One thread discussed improving their appearance through cosmetic surgery, dental work, hair plugs, and fasting to lose weight. *Wow!* An unexpected aspect. She wanted to respect these guys for trying so hard, but their hatred for women ran so deep their actions confused her. The idea of enduring dental work just so she could have sex with someone she hated didn't make much sense.

Scanning down, she abruptly stopped, stunned by a forum with the heading: *Kill 'Em All*. The posts aimed their hatred not just at women but at blacks, liberals, Jews, and Muslims, with calls for unspeakable violence. Overwhelmed, Dallas had to stop reading. Did the bureau have the resources to track down all these people? The cyber experts would probably say most of these guys were blowhards, cowards who talked smack online but in real life would melt in a confrontation with anyone. But current news reports indicated that at least a couple of these haters would act out their violent fantasies, leaving a trail of dead bodies.

Still feeling a little shaky, she logged back into the Not Normal forum. A few more incels had posted disgusting comments about college women. Their anger and hatred were so palpable it scared her. Not much else ever did. Dallas wasn't worried for herself, but for other women who might encounter these men. The women who had to sit by them at work every day, or exchange pleasantries with one at a family dinner. Or was this website the only place they let their true feelings show? Until they snapped one day and raped a woman or gunned downed twenty shoppers at a Wal-Mart.

Their rantings were so bizarre she realized there was no point in holding back and easing into the discussion. Time to make a direct request: *Whats the best school for finding girls to roofie?*

A few minutes later, a message from *Mas7erD3bator* appeared in her private inbox. *Dont post that shit here. But u can join our dark-web convo.*

Dallas quickly deleted her comment, not wanting to get kicked out, then tapped the link he'd posted. The new page seemed even more primitive, white text on a black background and narrow side margins. The header read *No Consent Needed*, and the chat section contained only two conversation threads. Both horrific, with comments such as: *Why is rape even a crime? If you roofie a roastie she doesn't remember.*

Taken aback, Dallas gulped half her beer and paced the room, trying to get her head into the part she had to play. But this role was unlike anything she'd ever done.

Finally she sat down and re-posted her comment in the private forum: *Whats the best school for finding girls to roofie?*

Mas7erD3bator quickly responded: *Congrats on taking the Black Pill. And welcome to non-normie sex options.*

She was in! Chatting with criminals. Success!

Yet being part of it made her sick. In the incel world, she'd learned that *taking the Black Pill* meant giving up on real relationships with women—but not giving up sex. These men resorted to prostitution, pornography, grab-and-go sexual assault, and sometimes rape.

Or worse . . . she soon discovered after reading through the forum. *KingCockXXX* had posted: *I know someone who kept a girl for years. They get used to it after a while.*

Dallas sucked in a harsh breath. *What the hell?* She finished her beer and paced the room until she felt calmer. Using her burner phone, she texted her FBI contact with a list of the profile names in the *roofie* forum and links to the *Kill 'Em All* thread. Concern abruptly set in. If someone without an invitation tried to access the page, would they shut it down? Fearing the worst, she sent her contact another text: *Be careful. Invitation only.*

She hoped the field office had cyber techs who could hack or engineer their way in. Dallas sat back, needing a break from the intensity. Her job was so strange! A sense of aloneness sent an ache through her body. She grabbed her personal cell phone, which didn't leave the hotel room, and called Cameron, who cut in with an auto-text: *Call you back in 5 minutes.*

The waiting frustrated her, so she wandered into the bedroom and planned what she would wear that evening. Cameron called while she was still pulling out clothes, so she dashed back and snatched up the cell. "Hey, Cam. How's the brewing business today?"

"Same old routine. Now I'm home and alone and missing you in the worst way."

"I miss you too. In fact, I plan to head straight to Flagstaff when I wrap up here." Hearing his voice had been all she needed for that decision.

"Fantastic!" A pause. "You'll stay a while so I can plan something special?"

"A few days at least. I'll see what the bureau says."

"I can't wait. How's your case going?"

"Good and bad. But I don't want to think about it." She shifted into sexy mode. "Tell me about your special plans."

"I'd rather surprise you. But it will involve a hot tub. Maybe under a snowy sky."

"You'll feed me chocolate-covered blueberries?"

"I'll eat some off your luscious body."

A surge of longing pulsed through her pelvis. "Hey, you're just torturing me now." Dallas glanced at the time. She had to start preparing for her first round as bait. "I'd better get back to work. Sorry, but I needed to hear your voice. I'll call you again when I can. Bye, love." She clicked off, feeling better . . . and strangely worse. The more time she spent with Cam, the more conflicted she became. But now was not the time to think about it. She had to get sexied up for the evening.

Excited for the change of pace, Dallas squeezed into a tight red dress and black strappy heels. She hated the shoes—because she couldn't run in them—but they seemed necessary for the part. For jewelry, she wore her favorite bureau-issued necklace, which disguised a tiny container of pepper spray as an artsy pendant, then remembered to tuck the tracker into her bra. For one more layer of protection, she dug out a black purse with a false bottom and slipped in her Glock 43, a deadly six-inch gun.

In the bathroom, she applied another layer of foundation and mascara—while vacillating about how she would get herself over to Tyler's Bar & Grill. She hadn't rented a car yet. Everywhere she needed to go was located within a small radius. Plus, hanging out in bars required her to drink. She was happy to make the sacrifice, but preferred not to drive. Without the stupid shoes, she would have just walked the ten blocks. But it could be a long night on her feet, so she opted for an Uber.

The crowded bar surprised her with decent music, a fusion band that blended rock and techno. Her favorites! She danced, drank a few microbrews, and flirted with a dozen college guys. She kept glancing around for Agent Keller, but didn't see her. Maybe the field office had sent someone else for backup. Dallas didn't care. In the moment, she felt like the luckiest person in the world—getting paid to have fun. Yet when she stepped outside at midnight to cool off, the dark aloneness reminded her that she risked her life on every undercover assignment. She'd been held hostage by an eco-terrorist with a bomb and had once been trapped in an underground bunker by survivalists who wanted to tear down the social structure and start over. The jeopardy this time had seemed less life-threatening, at least for her, but then she'd read the black-pill-incel comment about keeping a woman for years. The thought made her shudder and hurry back into the bar.

The band quit playing shortly after, so Dallas texted for an Uber. She would be doing this every evening until she caught the bastard, so she had to pace herself. All the attacks had happened between nine and eleven when the bars were most crowded . . . and that timeframe had passed.

As she moved toward the door, a drunk guy grabbed her and begged for a kiss. Dallas faked a laugh, shook free, and hurried away. Sometimes she hated men, but mostly she felt sorry for them. She liked sex as much as anyone, but she never let it guide her thinking or judgment. Dozens of prominent men had ruined their lives by letting their sexual needs dictate their behavior. *So pathetic!*

Back in her hotel room, she changed into a tank-top and got into bed with her laptop. Tired and sleepy, she planned to do a quick check of the incel sites and call it a night. In the main Not Normal forum, a new thread caught her eye: *Ending It All.*

Her pulse jumped. Were they talking about global annihilation? She opened the forum page and soon realized the subject was suicide. The posts were mostly brief and self-pitying, but some were tragic. One guy with a long lament had lost his parents in a car accident, then got fired for poor performance because of his grief. He claimed he'd never been on a date or had sex. Dallas ached for him. His loneliness was palpable, and he ended the message with: *I gonna shoot myself and be done.*

She had to respond.

As *bi*chgirlhater*, she clicked in the dialogue box and keyed in: *Please don't! Get counseling & join a support group. Maybe you'll meet someone.*

For a moment, she hesitated. The message was out of character for her online persona. Yet she had to try. He was human—and his pain touched her. She hit the return key and posted the message. Now she had to let it go. She couldn't afford the distraction.

Dallas shifted to the No Consent forum and glanced through the comments posted under her earlier question about "hooking up with easy fems."

Mas7erD3bator had posted: *btw, I lov WSU in Vancouver! Femoids r dumb as rocks and easy to roofie.*

Dallas sat upright, pulse accelerating. *Vancouver!* Was he the rapist?

Chapter 17

Friday, September 20, 5:45 a.m.

Jackson woke in a state of worry and conflict, already thinking about work. It seemed clear that Bettina Rios was either dead or in extreme danger. Also, her ex had been stalking her, assuming Aaron Russo was the intruder who'd run from her home. What the hell had he been doing in that house with Mrs. Rios, who'd been dead for days? Taking back things that belonged to him? Or picking up items for Bettina? The fact that Russo was still hanging around gave Jackson hope the young woman was alive somewhere. He desperately wanted to find her and protect her.

Yet he still had an unsolved homicide—with no solid idea of who the victim was. His team had been juggling the two cases, but Jackson decided he would focus on the missing woman until someone fully identified Carl . . . if they ever did.

Kera rolled over and snuggled up to him. "Will you pause the alarm before it goes off, please?"

He hit the button, then rolled back toward Kera, his body responding to her touch. Would they get away with this?

The bedroom door burst open, and two little boys rushed inside. "You're finally awake," Benjie said, standing next to the bed. "I've been waiting patiently and keeping Micah from bothering you."

Jackson sat up and hugged him. God, he loved this kind little soul. "Good morning, son." He loved saying that too.

Micah crawled between them and whined, "I want breakfast." The boy rolled over and kicked Jackson in the back.

"Hey, out of the bed," Jackson said gently. "You know the rules." He and Kera were entitled to at least one place that was off limits to the kids, and this bed was it.

Micah ignored him. Jackson glanced at Kera, but she didn't back him up. He stood and pulled on a shirt. "Everybody out while we get dressed. Please."

Benjie scooted toward the door, but his stepbrother didn't budge. Kera got up and coaxed Micah to move along. The boy wasn't happy about it and let them all know.

Jackson hoped Micah would grow out of this phase soon. As much as he wanted to love Kera's grandson and be a father to him, it just wasn't happening. Maybe if Kera and the boy hadn't been gone for so long to take care of her dying parents, things would be better between all of them. For a while, he'd thought she wasn't coming back.

With the kids out of the room, he closed the door. "Hey, sweetie. Let's try to be consistent with Micah on the bed issue. It's the only way he'll stop waking us up in the middle of the night."

"Can this wait until we've had coffee? I'm just not ready to have this discussion again." She sounded weary and sad.

Guilt flooded him, and Jackson stepped over and hugged her. She was so stoic he forgot sometimes that she was still grieving.

Later in the kitchen after they'd all had breakfast, he broached an even more difficult subject. "Kera, I need a favor."

She looked up from rising dishes in the sink. "What is it?"

"I need to see Bettina Rios' medical records from the clinic."

She shook her head, irritated. "You know I can't violate her privacy."

He'd expected that response but wasn't giving up. "If she's dead or in danger, which I'm pretty sure is the case, then she won't mind me looking at her chart, especially if it helps us find her."

"What if she's not in any kind of trouble? I could lose my job."

He was ready for that too. "If Bettina is alive and well, isn't she in breach of her contract? If she's trying to steal the baby, then you have an obligation to help the biological mother, who's also a client."

Kera narrowed her eyes at him. "Stop being so logical."

Jackson grinned. He'd made some headway. "I don't even need to see the file. Just a summary."

"I'll think about it."

"Thanks. I love you." Jackson kissed her and grabbed his jacket, moving on to the backup plan.

His first stop was North McKenzie Hospital where Erica Mather worked. She'd agreed to meet with him in the cafeteria. Kera had given him the woman's name and phone number the evening before, with her client's permission. Jackson took a seat in a corner of the busy room and waited, resisting the urge to buy a pastry. Finally a woman in pink scrubs approached him. Tall, with a long dark braid and bronze skin, she reminded him of a younger version of Kera. Jackson stood and introduced himself.

Erica shook his hand and flashed a nervous smile. "Thanks for looking into this for me. I'm worried sick about my baby."

Jackson was too, but he kept his face impassive. "Tell me everything you know about Bettina Rios."

"It's really not much. She's a very private person, and we only met face-to-face a few times."

No help. "Did she ever talk about her ex-boyfriend?"

"She mentioned him once but not by name."

"You don't know where he lives or works?"

Erica shook her head. "I do know that Bettina took care of her mother, who's diabetic and in a wheelchair. That's why she was doing the surrogacy. They needed money, and Bettina felt like she couldn't leave her mother alone to work a regular job."

Jackson hated to ask, but the information could be important. "Did she mention if they were in the country illegally?"

Erica pressed her lips together. "No, but I wondered."

If so, how had Bettina gotten through the screening at the fertility clinic? Was the fake driver's license they'd found all she needed? "Can I ask how much Bettina was paid?"

The question clearly made Erica uncomfortable, but she answered it. "She'll earn twenty thousand in total if she delivers the baby."

About what he'd expected. "How do the installments work?"

"She got a thousand up front, then a thousand a month pregnancy. She'll receive the whole second half when she hands over the baby." Erica choked up. "If she ever does."

Jackson wanted to know more, but he didn't want to upset the poor woman even further. "Have you been to her house?"

"Once. I gave her a ride to the clinic."

Jackson regretted making the trip out to the hospital. He'd wanted to meet this woman and size her up—just in case she had something to do with the surrogate's disappearance. Horrifying news stories indicated that when some women's maternal urges were in full swing anything was possible. But Erica Mather seemed straightforward and genuinely worried. Jackson reached for his wallet. "Sorry I took up your time." He handed her a business card. "If you think of anything that could be useful, call me." He stood, ready to leave.

So did Erica. "I don't know if this is important, but Bettina mentioned her mother was from Guatemala." She pressed her lips together. "I'm worried that's where she took the baby."

Jackson wanted to reassure her, but he didn't know what to say. His phone buzzed in his pocket. "Excuse me."

Erica nodded and walked away.

Jackson glanced at the screen. *Lammers*. What if she pressured him into conducting a press conference? He almost let the call go to voicemail, then answered at the last minute. "Hey, Sarge. What have you got?" He grabbed his coffee and headed for the elevator.

"Patrol officers picked up Aaron Russo and took him to an interrogation room. They said he put up a fight, so I'm calling Schak too."

Finally! A break in one of his cases.

Chapter 18

Jackson parked at the department and downed his lukewarm coffee. This would be another long day. He hoped he remembered to call Kera later. And Katie! He hadn't seen or spoken to his daughter recently. Now that she was working and taking community college classes, their paths rarely crossed. He tried to stay connected to Katie, but she was busy *adulting*, as she called it. As long as she stayed sober and out of trouble, he gave her a lot of slack. Still, he missed her.

Before getting out of the car, Jackson sent Katie a text: *Treat you to lunch at Bill & Tim's?* Their new favorite restaurant made the best ribs and coleslaw in town.

A few minutes later, he met Schak in the lobby outside the interrogation room. "Are you ready for this? Lammers says he's a fighter."

Schak pulled his stun gun. "As much as I love wrestling with thugs, my doc says those days are over."

Jackson laughed. "Just don't hit me with the damn thing." Schak had fully recovered from a heart attack he'd had on the job years earlier, but it had changed him. Jackson unlocked the door and stepped inside, with his partner right behind.

Head down on the table, the suspect looked asleep. His ankles were shackled together, and his wrists were cuffed behind his back.

At the sound of their steps, Russo jerked up. "What the fuck is happening? Why am I here?" He stood defiantly.

Schak bellowed, "Sit the hell down!"

The suspect froze and stared at Jackson, his eyes filled with accusation. "Why were you at Bettina's?"

Seriously? Jackson held back a snort. "Sit down. We're asking the questions."

Russo slowly eased into his chair.

"What were *you* doing there?" Jackson countered.

The man blinked and tightened his jaw. "I just stopped by to say hello. That's it. But Bettina wasn't home and Mrs. Rios was dead." He leaned over, straining against the cuffs behind his back. "I don't know what's going on, but I didn't do nuthin'. Why am I shackled like some kind of criminal?"

"Bettina says you abused her."

"That's a lie."

"And before that, two other women accused you of assault." Jackson kept it light. Those charges had been dropped; otherwise the suspect's record was clean.

"Liars!" Russo spat out the words. "I was never convicted."

Jackson decided to get what information he could before hitting the emotional part of the interrogation. Russo seemed unpredictable. "Where do you live?"

The suspect hesitated. "I'm kinda homeless right now. Why?"

Crap. They needed a place to search for Bettina. "Where do you sleep most of the time?"

"A friend's. Sometimes my car."

Jackson switched it up. "We know Bettina isn't here legally. Where's she from?"

"Guatemala. She applied for asylum, and they turned her down. Assholes."

Maybe her federal paperwork was accessible. Or maybe she'd gone back. Before Jackson could speak again, Russo banged his shackled feet together for effect. "What's this about? Why are you harassing me?"

Schak scoffed, purposefully loud. "Like you don't know. You assaulted the officers who brought you in. And you like to hit women. The question is: What did you do to Bettina this time?"

Russo's eyes went wide. "What do you mean? I haven't seen her."

His surprised expression seemed phony. Jackson wasn't impressed. "You were in her house. Why did you run?"

"Cops are assholes, so I knew you'd arrest me."

Time to pin him down. "Where were you last Saturday morning?"

The suspect looked confused. "Uh, I don't know. I think I was in Springfield."

"Doing what?"

"Sleeping." He shrugged. "I'm not a morning person."

Jackson's patience thinned. "No one has seen Bettina in nearly a week." He leaned forward and lowered his voice to a menace. "You're not leaving this room until you tell us where she is."

Panic flooded Russo's face. "What are you saying?"

"She went out for a run and never came back. We're confident you know why."

The suspect's eyes jumped around wildly, and he began to rock back and forth to a beat only he could hear. "No, no, no. This can't be true. She must have left town."

"And abandon her mother? She doesn't seem like that kind of person."

Russo broke into a high-pitched wail.

His anguish cut into Jackson like a knife. *Had he killed her?* Jackson pressed him further. "Did you know about the baby?"

"She's pregnant?" He sucked in a shocked breath. "Nooooo!" Russo threw himself out of the chair and against the wall. With his ankles shackled, he landed half sitting, half lying on the floor.

Jackson leapt to his feet.

Whap! Russo smashed his forehead against the concrete wall.

Jackson rushed around the table, as Schak drew his stun gun.

Whap! Blood oozed from the distressed man's nose.

Jackson grabbed Russo's shoulders and dragged him away from the wall.

"I can't live without Bettina!" Russo shouted. He began to beat his head on the floor.

What the hell? This guy needed a padded room and a shot of Thorazine.

"Clear!" Schak yelled.

Jackson jumped back, knowing Russo was about to be hit with fifty-thousand volts of electricity. The taser did the job, and the man lay quietly moaning. Now they just had to get him booked into the jail before he got worked up again.

"That was freaky," Schak said.

Jackson stared at the man on the floor. Was Russo just now coming to terms with what he'd done to Bettina—or was he disassociating? He'd acted like he believed someone else had abducted or killed his ex-girlfriend.

Chapter 19

Friday, 12:10 p.m.

Dallas sat on a bench in a quaint little park, eating a blueberry bagel she'd bought at a nearby deli. Agent Keller had wanted to meet in person again. The clandestine setup probably wasn't necessary. She wasn't deep undercover, and her target was unlikely to have access to her communications. She and Keller could have talked on their phones, but the personal connection was nice after being alone in her hotel room for days. Not counting her session at the bar the night before.

A few minutes later, Keller joined her, wearing jeans, a man's jacket, and a knit cap. Her contact was way overdressed for the sunny fall day, but that was often the nature of the job. "Mind if I sit here?"

"Go ahead." Dallas resisted a smile. "Nice day, huh?"

"I'm feeling it." Keller sat rather close and didn't speak for a while. Finally she took out a cell and scrolled through the photos. "You've got to see this." She turned the phone and displayed an image, then whispered, "Brett Thorton."

Thirtyish, with a dark-blond receding hairline. Thorton also had a large nose, close-set eyes, and acne scars. No wonder the guy had trouble getting laid on his own. Human beings only tolerated micro deviations of facial symmetry and proportionality in their appraisal of beauty. Everyone else had to be charming or rich to attract a partner.

On the upside, bureau cyber techs had clearly been successful in tracking the identity of *Mas7erD3bator* in the twelve hours since she'd sent them the lead. Now they had to catch him in the act. A judge would never issue a search warrant with the flimsy intel they had, and the access might not produce any real evidence.

Dallas finished her bagel, then whispered, "Social media?"

Keller shifted closer. "Yes. I'll get eyes on him today to confirm his appearance."

Dallas glanced at her own phone just to look casual. "Background?"

"Nada."

That could be good or bad. Thorton either was a first-time offender or too smart to have been caught before. "What else?"

"The Pit Stop."

The bar where the second assault had taken place. "Tonight at eight."

The agent nodded and slipped her phone into a pocket. "See you around." She rose and walked away.

Dallas waited another few minutes, then walked back to her hotel room to check out Thorton's social media sites. She friended him through her Amber Facebook page and posted about hitting the scene at the Pit Stop later. If that didn't bait the trap, then nothing would.

Chapter 20

Friday, 12:25 p.m.

Jackson walked into Bill & Tim's and inhaled deeply. The smoky aroma of BBQ sauce combined with the comforting smell of French fries made his mouth water. He was also meeting Katie. Lunch didn't get much better than this. Usually, he ate a cold turkey sandwich at his desk.

As he stood in the foyer waiting, he tried to put his worry about Bettina Rios aside. There was nothing else he could do at the moment. A White Bird crisis team had escorted Aaron Russo to the county jail, where he'd been medicated, placed in solitary confinement, and would be evaluated by a psychiatrist "soon."

His team had notified law enforcement agencies and media stations across the state to be on alert for the missing woman. Getting Bettina's photo out to the public gave them the best shot at finding her. Jackson had even requested that a search-and-rescue team comb the neighborhood. He didn't know when that would happen, but Schak and Evans were out there now, talking to neighbors. *It was okay to take a break to eat and connect with his daughter,* he told himself.

A moment later, Katie walked in behind him. "Hey, Dad. Good timing." The sight of her as a grown woman—who had the dark-haired beauty of his ex-wife but without the scowl—still startled him sometimes. She'd grown three inches in the last year and started working as a food server. Bought a car too, with a little of his help. Jackson stepped in for a hug.

She indulged him with a quick, one-armed squeeze. "Let's order. I have to be back at the college in an hour."

"Okay." He stepped toward the counter. The place was a mix of service styles, with the menu on the wall. He knew exactly what he wanted. "Half order of ribs and French fries, please." He turned to Katie. "I'll have a salad for dinner to balance out the calories."

She laughed. "Yeah, and I'm going to give up peanut butter cups."

"Don't even say that! I'll have to disown you."

Katie ordered ribs and coleslaw, and Jackson handed over his credit card. He figured he would be paying for whatever restaurant meals they ate together for the rest of their lives—a parent thing.

They found a table by the window, and he sat facing the entrance. "What class do you have next at school?"

"Biology, then basic design. I hope to find a way to be creative. I'm just not sure how yet."

She'd changed her mind a few dozen times already. "Great. Keep exploring until you find something you love."

"But I like everything, except math. That's the problem."

"You'll figure it out." Their interaction felt like she'd already moved out and they were catching up. Would he ever be ready for that?

"Mom was good with numbers."

Jackson tensed. Katie never talked about her mother, which suited him fine. His part in Renee's death still tormented both of them, and he hoped his daughter wouldn't go there. "Yeah, she loved spreadsheets and lists. But that's not something you can inherit."

"Do you ever think about her?"

"Of course." He reached across and squeezed Katie's hand. "I'll never forgive myself for what happened."

She looked at him, eyes watering. "You should. I've forgiven you. I know you were manipulated."

Her forgiveness made his heart swell. "Thank you for saying that." Still, the fact that a criminal had tricked him still stung. He should have moved slower and questioned what he was seeing.

"Micah keeps waking me up in the middle of the night," Katie said, cutting into his thoughts. "It's really bugging me. Can you do something about it?"

"It's not good for me either. Maybe Kera and I will talk to a pediatrician."

A server brought their food and they both dug in, eating with their fingers. After a moment, Katie put down her ribs. "I think I have to break up with Ethan."

Yes! Stalling, Jackson finished his bite and grabbed a napkin. This was tricky territory. He wanted to encourage her to follow through, but he couldn't openly criticize her boyfriend—in case they stayed together. He wasn't even sure why he didn't like Ethan. "He's not working out for you?"

"He's too controlling."

A trickle of fear rolled down his spine. Jackson vowed to stay calm and casual. He couldn't afford to alienate his daughter again. That time when she'd run away—and been out of control—had been the worst of his life. "How so?"

"A lot of little stuff. Like he wants me to wear dresses more often. And he always has to drive, even though it's my car." She rolled her eyes. "He gets jealous over stupid little things too."

Jackson struggled to keep his voice measured. "Katie, sweetheart. Those are all red flags. Trust your instincts on this one. He's not right for you." *Or anyone.* The urge to find the abuser-in-training and warn him to stay the hell away pulsed in Jackson's veins. But Katie was an adult, and he had to trust her to handle the situation. She had already figured the guy out after a few months of dating. Yet if Ethan's behavior escalated even a little, Jackson would show him how much fun it was to date a cop's daughter. If the guy hadn't thought about those possibilities, he was too stupid for words.

"I know," Katie said, conflicted now. "But he can be so sweet. I hate to hurt his feelings."

Now Jackson understood. Her big heart was getting in the way, and she'd come to him for tough love. "Give Ethan the band-aid treatment. Just tear him off and go on with your life. He'll be fine."

"I know." She sighed, picked up her ribs, and ripped off a chunk of meat with her teeth.

Jackson resisted the urge to laugh. The women in his life were sweet on the surface, but if you crossed them you got chewed up and spit out.

As he walked into his work cubicle, Jackson's desk phone rang, startling him. Only his bosses called that line. He sucked in a breath and picked up the handheld receiver.

"Hey, Jackson. It's Davenport in PR."

A flash of hope. "What have you got?"

"A lead on your shooting victim."

Finally! "Who is he?"

"No last name yet, but the tipster thinks Carl used to be

her paper boy."

Huh. A gig job that required no skill and little public contact. "What's the caller's name and number?"

"She wanted to remain anonymous, but she sounded quite sure of her information."

"Thanks." Jackson set down the phone. Time to switch gears and focus on the homicide case. This was the new norm. Everyone in the Violent Crimes Unit juggled multiple investigations to keep up with Eugene's rising crime rate. He briefly considered calling Sophie and asking her to check out Carl's newspaper employment, but thought better of it. Sometimes the right questions could open up new lines of investigation. He needed to do this himself, and he wanted the information right now. He jumped up, glad to be moving again. Sitting at his desk was too frustrating.

He pulled into the *Willamette News*, only the second time he'd been to their new location. The massive parking lot was less than a third full. Jackson walked toward the windowless three-story structure that housed their huge printing press. Like everyone else in town, he wondered how long the media company would keep cranking out a daily paper.

The production office between the two buildings didn't have a receptionist and smelled like ink. Jackson stuck his head into the nearest open door. A man about his age sat behind a desk, wearing a short-sleeved shirt. As he looked up, his pudgy face glistened with sweat. "Can I help you?"

"I hope so." Jackson introduced himself.

"Ron Haden, production manager." He stood and reached out his hand.

Jackson shook it, then got right down to business. "I need to identify a victim, and one of your customers says he used to deliver her newspaper." Jackson held out his phone with Carl's image showing.

Haden scowled. "He's dead?"

"Yes. We think his name is Carl. Do you recognize him?"

Haden shook his head. "No, but the crew boss might. Let's go ask."

They stepped through swinging doors into a long narrow room with a roll of newsprint laid out down the middle.

"Jeanie!" Haden yelled over the noise of the press next door. An older woman with a bandana over her hair looked up from her proofing task and walked over.

Jackson introduced himself again and held out the photo. "Do you recognize this man?"

She leaned in. "I think he had a route for a short time." Squinting now, she shuddered. "He looks dead. What happened?"

"Someone shot him. We think his first name is Carl. Do you know his last name?"

"Not off the top of my head, but I can find out. He was here last summer." She stepped over to her standing desk, tapped a computer icon, and waited for files to load. After a minute of searching, she looked back to Jackson. "Carl Jagger."

Relieved, he jotted down the name. "What else can you tell me about him?"

She wagged her head slowly back and forth, thinking hard. "He wasn't here long, and he was late a lot. Then one day, he just didn't show up. But I was gonna fire him anyway. My crew has to perform or they're out."

Paper routes were crappy jobs, but this lady took her supervisor role seriously. Jackson pressed forward. "Do you have information about his next of kin?"

She sighed. "I'll check." Jeanie spent another few minutes

in the database, then jotted something on a sticky note and handed it to Jackson. "Carl didn't list a name on the emergency contact line, but this is the number and address he gave for himself. Good luck." She went back to proofreading.

Jackson thanked her and left.

In his car, he glanced at the information again. Feeling less than optimistic, he called the number, which was answered by a young girl who claimed to not know Carl Jagger. Jackson pulled out his tablet and entered the victim's name into the department database but came up with nothing. He had the same experience on Facebook and Instagram. Even spelling Carl with a K didn't help. Nobody local with that name had an obvious social media profile. *Crap!*

He texted the update to his teammates and asked Evans to check more sites. She knew about a bunch of others, but he'd never had any luck with them. Determined to find the victim's family—if he had one—Jackson drove to the address, a small house in the Bethel area, and knocked. A dog barked aggressively until a fifty-something woman opened the door a few inches. Clinging to a walker, she shushed the little mutt, then snapped at Jackson. "What do you want?"

"I'm looking for Carl Jagger's family."

"Never heard of him." She started to close the door.

Jackson stuck his foot out to catch it. "I'm with Eugene Police. This is important."

"I still can't help you."

"How long have you lived here?"

"Almost a year."

Maybe the victim had moved after he left his paper route. "What's your landlord's name?"

She looked wary.

"This isn't about you. I need to find Carl Jagger's next of kin."

"I'll be back." The woman closed the door.

While Jackson waited, a train rolled by less than a block away, the noise deafening. After a few minutes, the occupant came back, holding an envelope. "The owner is Randy Stoops, and this is where I mail my rent check." She pointed to the address label and a scribbled phone number, and Jackson made a note. "Thanks." He walked away, feeling like he'd wasted his time again.

Back in his car, he called Stoops and left a message, asking for his help.

Chapter 21

Friday, 1:35 p.m.

Sophie Speranza stared at her mostly blank screen. She was supposed to be writing a follow-up story about the dead man with the gunshot wound—except she didn't have any new details. The police department's spokesperson claimed they didn't even know his name. *Strange!* The crime definitely intrigued her. How the hell had his body ended up in the road? She picked up her phone to call Jackson, but changed her mind. She'd already left him a couple of messages.

Sophie got up from her desk, made mint tea in the tiny break area, and chatted with a co-worker before getting back to writing. Without real facts, she'd have to speculate. The plastic wrap indicated the killer was somewhat methodical, or at least worried about getting blood in his home or vehicle. She typed a sentence to that effect and paused, wondering if the medical examiner had found any trace evidence.

She reached for her phone to call Jasmine, then stopped mid-air. Anguish slammed into Sophie's chest, and she breathed deeply to get control. Jasmine had broken up with her . . . and broken her heart. Sophie had never loved anyone like she loved Jas, but she was determined to move on. Her girlfriend had let fear ruin their relationship. She'd been afraid of coming out to her parents from the beginning, then

Jasmine had worried that her peers in the public safety department would find out she was not only gay, but involved with a journalist. *Oh the horror!*

Sophie sighed. Not only did she miss their evenings together, she'd lost her inside-information source. As she started to call the medical examiner's office, footsteps sounded behind her. She spun in her chair.

Hoogstad, her boss, stood in the opening to her cubicle. Fifty, fatter than ever, and balding, he leaned against the frame, breathing hard. She tried not to judge him, but he obviously didn't care about his health or appearance. Rumor was that he'd been a bachelor his whole life. "Hey, Sophie, there's a breaking crime story in west Eugene. I need you out there now."

She popped out of her chair, pulse racing. "What's happening?"

"A kidnapping. A woman in the Target parking lot was boxed in by two cars, then taken at gunpoint."

"Holy shit!" She grabbed her camera and shoved it into her purse. "Anything else?"

"No, that's your job." Hoogstad stepped aside and gestured for her to move along.

She didn't need to be encouraged. Sophie bolted out of her workspace and down the stairs. She ran past the rented offices where the journalists used to sit before half were laid off, then turned toward the exit.

Outside, she picked up her pace, glad she'd worn pants and sneakers today. She climbed into her Scion, mentally mapping the fastest route. As she backed out, Sophie spotted a familiar face coming out of the print office. *Was that Jackson?* What the hell was he doing out here? For a moment, she let off the accelerator, tempted to drive over and ask him.

But a kidnapping in progress meant every minute counted. Especially if she wanted to speak to a witness or get a decent photo. She could always call Jackson later. Or just ask the production department what he'd wanted. Sophie hit the gas and raced out of the parking lot.

By the time she reached the Target store at the opposite end of town, the patrol cars were gone. No crime scene tape either, but a small group of customers stood near a cart-return enclosure, talking about what had just happened. Sophie took their names and statements, but the information was slim. A young, dark-haired woman had got into her car, then had quickly been boxed in on both sides by two other vehicles. Men had been behind the wheel in both. One guy had run to the victim's car and smashed in the driver's side window. Once he had the door open, he'd climbed in and shoved the woman over, then drove off with her.

The witnesses had conflicting reports about what happened next. But clearly, all three vehicles had left the parking lot, suggesting there were at least three people involved in the kidnapping. Sophie took a picture of the group with the store's entrance showing prominently in the background, then hustled inside to ask the manager about surveillance footage. He declined to comment or assist her. Knowing she'd hit the end of what she could learn at the scene, she headed back to the newspaper. If she wrote fast, she might make the deadline for the morning edition.

On the drive, the kidnapping troubled her. The crime had happened in a public parking lot in broad daylight. *So blatant!* That wasn't all that nagged at her. Another Eugene woman had been missing for a week. Bettina Rios had gone out for a run and never come back. The story and photo had hit the TV news stations late the night before and again this morning. The women were both twenty-something, petite, and dark-haired. Were the abductions connected? If so, what the hell was happening?

Sophie put in her earpiece and called Jackson, still curious about what he'd been doing at the newspaper that morning. As usual, she had to leave a message and hope he would call her back. But she wouldn't let any of it go. Women's lives were at risk.

At four-thirty, she shut down her computer and hurried through the building to the printing department. She zoomed past the manager's office and headed straight into the proofing area. Jeanie would know. The production assistant's job kept her in contact with just about everyone who worked there. Sophie found her at her desk in the proofing room.

"Hey, Jeanie."

She looked up. "Sophie! What brings you out here?"

"I'm writing a follow-up story about the homicide victim. The guy wrapped in plastic."

"Oh yeah. I saw your first piece." She laughed. "But I didn't actually read it."

Sophie flashed a fake smile. "I'm a little short on details. So hey, I saw Detective Jackson leaving this building earlier and really need to know what that was about."

Jeanie broke into a smile. "The victim worked here last summer as a carrier. Want to know his name?"

"Please! That would be very helpful."

"Carl Jagger. I didn't remember much about him at first, but after the detective left I started thinking. Carl was a good-looking guy, except for his teeth, and somebody said he used to live in Costa Rica." Jeanie pushed the bandana off her hair and used it to wipe her brow. "I couldn't handle that kind of heat. It's bad enough here in the warm months."

Interesting, but not enough. "Anything else?"

"Nope, but if you want to know more, you should ask the bundle haulers. He was pretty friendly with a guy named Sam."

Chapter 22

Friday, 4:25 p.m.

Jackson trudged into the department, wishing he'd bought a cup of decent coffee while he was out and about. He settled for a Diet Dr. Pepper out of the vending machine and sat down at his desk. Feeling like he'd hit another dead end with the homicide, Jackson focused on Bettina Rios again.

He'd assigned Schak the work of searching her and her mother's financial and phone records. A tedious task, but over the years his partner had gotten quite good at spotting both patterns and irregularities. Evans handled paperwork equally well, but she got bored and hated it. He'd asked her to track down the missing woman's acquaintances. Neither detective had come up with anything helpful.

Bettina Rios seemed as off the grid as the murder victim. Millions of people lived their lives openly, often in excruciating detail, on social media sites, yet others operated completely in the shadows, barely making an impression in the social fabric.

What his team still didn't know about the missing woman was her medical history and the details of her surrogacy contract. Not wanting to ask his girlfriend in person, Jackson texted Kera: *You said you would think about it. Did you check Bettina's file?* He pressed send, then quickly followed with:

No pressure. At this point, he didn't expect the information to be helpful.

A minute later, his phone showed a message from Kera: *Nothing in Bet's file will help you. Sorry.*

Just as he'd thought. Jackson realized he hadn't checked his work email since that morning, so he opened the software. A message from the pathologist with a PDF attached stood out in bold as unopened. Jackson downloaded the report and skimmed the results of Serena Rios' autopsy. The woman had died of a heart attack, likely triggered by stress and dehydration. Her extremities also showed signs of neuropathy, brought on by high blood sugar—untreated diabetes.

Jackson felt strangely relieved that Aaron Russo hadn't killed her. Or at least not directly. But if the ex-boyfriend had abducted or murdered Bettina—leaving her disabled mother without a caregiver—then he'd contributed to her death. It wasn't a charge the DA would ever file. Too hard to prove. They had to connect Russo to Bettina's death first. *Or disappearance,* Jackson reminded himself. She could still be alive somewhere.

He stood and stretched, trying to make up his mind. He wanted to go home for dinner and see Benjie . . . and Kera. But Micah had been so cranky lately that Jackson decided to skip the potential chaos and keep working. Still, he needed to eat, so he grabbed his jacket and satchel and headed out.

A Five Guys cheeseburger wolfed down in their parking lot gave Jackson the most pleasure he'd had in a week. The thought made him laugh. A few minutes later, as he drove toward River Road, a vague depression set in. Was living with Kera and Micah making him unhappy? *Oh hell.* Did he need to see a counselor?

Jackson turned down the dead-end street where the

missing woman had lived and parked in front of her house. The crime-scene tape he'd strung across the door flapped in the warm evening breeze. Another search of Bettina's personal things could wait. He crossed to the neighbor's house instead, and rapped loudly. A car was in the driveway and a TV played inside.

Karen Silas opened the door, her surprise turning into a smile. "Detective Jackson. Hello."

"Sorry to bother you at dinner time."

"It's all right. My husband is out picking up a to-go order from Twin Dragon. So we have a few minutes. Come in."

Jackson stepped inside, blinking at the canary-yellow walls. Too long in here and he would have a seizure. He held out his phone with an image of Aaron Russo showing. "Have you ever seen this man?"

She pulled glasses up to her face and nodded. "I think he might live around here. I saw him walking out on the street once, and last week he was sitting in a car."

Jackson's pulse quickened. "What day did you see him?"

"Maybe Saturday." The woman suddenly sucked in her breath. "Did he kidnap Bettina?"

Jackson was starting to think so. "Possibly. What kind of vehicle was he in?"

"Oh dear, let me think. It was red and kind of sporty, but I don't recognize particular makes or models. Sorry."

"You're doing fine. Where was the car parked?"

"Around the corner on Lombard, down by Fir Lane where you enter the neighborhood."

A tingle ran up Jackson's spine. Lots of bushy trees and places to hide there, and Russo had likely known about Bettina's morning-run habit. Anxious to get going, Jackson put away his phone and asked, "Anything else you can tell me?"

"No. I'm sorry I didn't mention this before." The neighbor choked up, about to cry. "I should have told Bettina when I first saw the guy. But she only mentioned her ex-boyfriend once and never said he was stalking her."

"She might not have known." Jackson thanked her again and stepped back outside.

The quick drive around the corner felt silly, but a woman's life could be at stake. Jackson stopped near the park entrance, got out, and looked around. The trees on the left provided plenty of cover.

But was Bettina still alive?

Statistics suggested she was not. Possessive abuser types often killed their ex-partners rather than "allow" them to get involved with anyone else. His heart skipped a beat as he realized his daughter was about to be in that situation. Maybe he should personally monitor Katie's break-up to keep her safe. *Oh hell.* How thin could he spread himself? At this point, he had to stay focused on a crime that had happened.

Jackson walked to the cluster of trees and scanned the ground. The foliage debris was too thick to conduct a simple visual search. The setting sun left the area mostly shaded too. He called Gunderson.

The ME surprised him by answering. "I'm sure I don't know yet, but you can ask." His voice was so dry it cracked.

"I need a couple of techs out here by the entrance to Maurie Jacobs Park. I think Bettina Rios might have been kidnapped right here."

"Is she related to Serena Rios? The autopsy we did this morning?"

Oh right. He hadn't been involved in the case yet. "Her daughter. She disappeared last Saturday, most likely from this area."

"That's tragic for the family, but we're overwhelmed."

He wanted Jackson to volunteer his own team, but they didn't have the manpower. "So are we. I've got three detectives working a homicide and a missing woman. I'm focused on her. She could be alive somewhere, possibly captive."

"You win. I'll send the intern out to the area first thing in the morning."

Jackson's shoulders slumped in relief. "Thanks." He didn't have time to spend the evening on his hands and knees searching for . . . likely nothing.

Back in his car, he checked his notes. Russo had claimed to be homeless even though he'd had a driver's license with an address on it when they searched him. Time to check out that house. They might need a warrant, and he'd get one if necessary. But since the suspect was in jail, it wouldn't hurt to stop by his place and check out the situation.

Jackson called Evans. "You got anything on Bettina Rios yet?"

"No." Frustration in her voice. "I found her on Facebook earlier as part of Russo's page, but she doesn't have one of her own, and her Instagram contacts are mostly in Guatemala. Also no work history I can find."

Jackson shared her frustration. The surrogacy money Bettina earned might be enough to live on, and if she and her mother were here illegally, that might be all they had.

"Without a phone or place of employment," Evans continued, "I'm really struggling to find anyone who knows her."

"Whoever targeted her may have counted on that to get away with it."

"I'm assuming Russo is still in jail?"

"Yes. I'm headed to the address we found on his driver's license."

"Text it to me, and I'll meet you."

"Thanks. See you soon."

Chapter 23

In the wavering shadows of twilight, the house gave Jackson a shiver. Boarded over windows, rusty shopping carts covered with black plastic, and a stink he could smell from the sidewalk. Marijuana with an undertone of clogged toilet.

He climbed back in his car, accessed his tablet, and plugged the address into the database. Yep, the department had received nine reports about the residence in the past year. Jackson called dispatch, asking for patrol units. "I just need them out front, ready to respond."

Evans arrived a minute later and parked behind him. As they stood by her car, staring at the place from an angle, she groaned. "God, I hope that poor woman is not in there."

"I called for backup. As soon as we spot them, we'll approach." Jackson reached under his jacket and touched his Sig Sauer. "I have a bad feeling about this."

"No shit." Evans shook off some tension. "Do we have probable cause to enter without permission?"

"We will soon."

Lights at the end of the block caught his attention. A big SUV. "Let's go." Jackson started toward the door with Evans in step beside him. The dark house suddenly came alive—bustling with the sounds of footsteps running and furniture being dragged.

A porch light came on, and a man stepped outside. "What are you doing here?" Bearded, thin, and shirtless, he wasn't intimidating on the surface.

Jackson stopped at the wood platform that served as an entry. "We're looking for Aaron Russo, and we know he lives here." If his roommates knew Russo was in custody, they would be more wary.

"Aaron never actually lived here. We only let him sleep on the couch. He also had his mail sent here, but that was months ago."

Disappointing, but possibly true. A lot of young men were sofa surfers. "Where does Aaron stay now?"

"I don't know. I haven't seen him."

That, Jackson didn't believe. "Do you know Bettina Rios?"

The shirtless man stuffed his hands into his pockets. "Who's that?" he finally asked.

"A missing woman." Jackson stepped onto the platform, eye level with the man now and invading his space. "What's your name?"

"Brad Zimmer. Who are you?"

"Detective Jackson, Eugene Police. I'd like to come in."

"I can't let you do that." The flickering yellow porch light cast his face in a weird glow.

"A woman is missing, and Aaron Russo was stalking her. We have reason to think she's in this house."

"She's not."

"Then let us take a fast look. We're not here to bust you for drugs." Jackson shrugged. "But if we come back with a warrant, we'll search every single stash spot."

Zimmer's eyes flitted around as he considered it. "I'll let her come in," he said, nodding at Evans, "but not you."

Evans started to speak, but Jackson cut her off. "I think I

hear someone calling for help. Step aside."

A vehicle idled on the street behind him. A new patrol unit. Jackson recognized the sound of the special-order engine.

"Oh fuck." The guy opened the door and yelled inside the house. "They're coming in!"

Frantic footsteps pounded. A window on the side jerked opened, and someone grunted as he climbed out.

Zimmer finally moved aside, pleading, "You said a quick look."

Jackson moved slowly into the dark, dank space. Only a single bulb glowed in the hall.

"Lights please," Evans called out behind him.

Zimmer scooted past and flipped a switch in the kitchen. "That's all we have working."

Hand on his weapon, Jackson glanced around the ten-by-ten living room. Two ratty couches, coffee cans filled with cigarette butts, clothes and jackets piled everywhere, and crusty food plates. A fog of smoke, both tobacco and pot, saturated the air. *Home sweet home.*

Only one guy remained, passed out on the big couch.

Jackson eased into the kitchen. So much crap covered the counters he couldn't process it all, but the kitchen table was suspiciously clear. That must be where they weighed, cut, or snorted their drugs. Someone had cleaned it off in a hurry.

The property had no garage, so the kitchen was a closed space. The house had to have a back door; city code required it. Jackson intended to check the yard and any sheds or structures that might be out there. Beside him, Evans made a disgusted sound in her throat and went back into the living area.

Jackson followed as she entered the dim hall, which was

just a foyer for three doors. Two bedrooms and a bathroom, he assumed. Evans stepped through an open door into a tiny dark bedroom. Jackson checked the second bedroom, trying not to gag on the stink of sweat. He scanned the tiny closet, crammed so full of backpacks, purses, and clothes, there wasn't room for anything else. Probably all stolen.

Holding his breath, he threw open the bathroom door, cringed at the wet towels on the floor around the toilet, and backed out. A moldy shower curtain stood open, revealing the bathtub to be empty.

"I'm going outside," Evans called from the other bedroom.

Jackson hustled past Zimmer, who stood in the hall watching, and followed Evans out a narrow door into the backyard.

A metal shed sat off to the side, surrounded by overstuffed garbage bags. Moonlight glinted on a padlock. Jackson turned to Zimmer, who stayed with them. "Unlock it."

"I don't have the key. The guy who does isn't here."

"Then we'll bust it down. This must be where I heard the call for help."

Zimmer sighed. "There's no one in there, I promise. Just a bunch of stuff."

Likely more stolen items. "We're not leaving until we see it." The house itself was full of addicts and thieves, but Jackson seriously doubted he would find Bettina here.

Unless there was a hidden room somewhere.

Chapter 24

Friday, 8:45 p.m.

Wearing a snug purple dress with peek-a-boo side cutouts, Dallas strode into the Pit Stop, heels clicking. Several men turned to stare. She flashed a few smiles and made her way to the bar. Guys at the counter snuck glances too, a few seeming surprised.

Arriving alone wasn't typical female behavior. Most college women, maybe all females, went out in pairs or groups. "Safety in numbers," they'd all been taught from an early age. She didn't have a wing woman, which should work to her favor. A predator would more likely choose a victim who didn't have a support group.

A man approached before she could even order. "Can I buy you a drink?"

He was gorgeous! Dallas couldn't help but smile. In another time and place . . . "Thanks, but I've got this." She pivoted to the bartender, another college-aged guy. "I'll have a small Fest." The local microbrew listed on the Specials board.

Pleased to discover that the beer was a hearty brown-sugar color, she took her drink to the last open table. Smaller than Tyler's, the tavern's back wall hosted three dartboards, and musicians were setting up near a tiny stage in the corner. No dance floor though.

After an hour of nursing her beer, chatting with people, and doing her best to ignore the whiny folk guitar, Dallas spotted Brett Thorton walk in. His red nylon jacket strained to stay zipped over his thick belly, and he had pulled what was left of his hair into a short ponytail. Not a good look.

He stopped in the middle of the room and scanned the tables, searching like a predator. Dallas glanced down, not ready to make eye contact. He had to come to her.

And he did. A few minutes later, he sauntered over with a beer in hand. "Can I use this chair?" he asked, his voice uneven. "There's nowhere else to sit."

He was nervous. Even after six victims. "Uh, yeah, I guess so." She had to play this just right. If she was too friendly, he might think he had a chance without drugging her. If she was too standoffish, he would target someone easier.

"Thanks. My name's Adam."

Giving a phony name, a sure sign of malicious intent. Dallas flipped her hair back, acting the part. "I'm Amber." She glanced around. "Is it always this crowded?"

"This is nothin'." He scooted his chair to the table, making himself at home. "First time here?"

"No, but it's been a while. I had to get serious about my studies."

"What's your major?"

She wanted to say 'criminal justice' to see the look on his face, but she resisted. "Sustainable public policy."

"Huh?" He squinted but obviously didn't want to admit he had no idea what that meant.

Dallas explained. "Someday, I'll be an unappreciated government worker who tries to mitigate the effects of global warming by crafting smart guidelines." She immediately regretted her choice, wishing she'd just said 'teacher.'

Thorton laughed to the point of rudeness.

Dallas hoped she had an opportunity to punch him later. "Someone has to care." She started to get up, make him chase her a little.

He grabbed her arm, but quickly let go. "Hey, sorry. I didn't mean anything. I thought you were trying to be funny."

"I kind of was." She eased back down and gave him a soft smile. "I know it's not a cool career, but I may save the planet." She winked and picked up her beer.

Surprised, he raised his too and they clinked glasses.

"To bureaucratic heroes," she said, thinking of all the FBI analysts who spent their lives staring at computer screens to stop people like Thorton.

After a moment of quiet, he said, "You're pretty enough to be a model."

"Thank you."

Behind him, Agent Keller walked by, dressed in the same male clothes she'd worn earlier.

Relieved, Dallas decided it was time. "Will you excuse me?" She paused. "And watch my beer while I'm gone?"

"Sure." He spoke casually, but his eyes glinted.

Dallas hurried toward the matching doors next to the bar counter, feeling the weight of her weapon in the purse hanging from her shoulder. Both bathrooms were unisex, so one was open. She slipped in and locked the door behind her. Her phone beeped, and she pulled it from her handbag. Keller had texted: *He just drugged your drink. Let's play this out.*

Oh yeah. She was on board. Catching Thorton in the act would force him to plead guilty to at least some of the other assaults. Dallas texted back: *I'm in.*

She stalled for a moment, then headed back to her table. Thorton smiled when she sat down. *Devious asshole.* Dallas grinned back. He had no idea who he was fucking with. She picked up her half-full glass of beer, which showed no signs of being tampered with. "Do you like this music?"

"Not really." He made a face.

"Me neither. Will you go ask them to play something danceable?"

"Uh, I don't think they take requests."

"Oh, come on. It's worth trying." She reached over and stroked his forearm. "Maybe we'll slow dance."

He tightened his mouth and nodded, as though trying to talk himself into it.

Dallas took a sip—held it in her throat—and waved him off.

Thorton finally walked away. She pulled her purse into her lap and turned to face the wall. She opened the plastic bag inside, leaned over, and spit the beer into it. She left the ziplock open for the moment and shifted back to the table. Her target stood next to a guitar player, talking. Both men glanced over at her, so she waved.

When they looked away, she did too. Dallas dumped the rest of her drink into the container. Zipping it closed sloshed the liquid and got her purse wet. Her hidden gun would be fine, but the burner phone wouldn't like the moisture. She snatched it out, turned back to the table, and checked for messages. None.

Dallas looked around and saw Keller leaning against a wall by the back exit. Her backup was in position. Dallas hoped Keller had called in additional agents after spotting their suspect.

Thorton returned to the table. "They said the next song will have a dance beat."

Dallas beamed. "Thanks."

He nodded at her empty glass. "Do you want another one?"

"Oh no. I've already had too many."

Keller would likely send someone over to retrieve her glass as soon as they left the table. The glass would have Thorton's fingerprints and traces of the drug he'd used. Forensic evidence for court.

They chatted about their favorite bands until the new song started. Dallas stood and slowed her speech, the way a drunk would. "This one isn't great, but it's better." She took a step toward the musicians and staggered. She giggled, glanced at Thorton, and slurred, "After this, I'd better go home."

The predator followed her up to the stage. While Dallas danced, stumbling awkwardly, he stood by, grinning like a guy in a strip club. Other people watched too, but as the only one dancing, she wasn't surprised. Near the end of the song, she staggered again and pretended to fall against Thorton. "I need to get out of here," she mumbled. "I feel dizzy."

"Did you walk?" He put an arm around her, leading in the direction of the back door.

"Yeah. My apartment's"—Dallas paused and forced a hiccup—"nearby." She touched her pepper-spray pendant to make sure it was accessible and staggered toward the rear exit.

Outside, she pulled in breaths of fresh air. Thorton's grip on her arm tightened, and he guided her across the dark parking lot.

"I live . . . the other way." She acted too drunk to enunciate.

Thorton pulled her arm and pointed at a big vehicle in the back corner. "I'll give you a ride. You're too hammered to walk."

When they reached the Tahoe, he opened the backseat door. "You should lay down while I drive. You'll feel better."

Dallas hesitated. *How far did she have to play this?* Long enough for him to touch her sexually or grab at her underclothes. She stepped toward the open car door.

In a sudden move, he pushed her hard with both hands. Dallas fell face first onto the backseat. As she landed, he shoved a hand between her legs, lifting her hips into the vehicle. Every fiber in her body wanted to roll over and fight him. But she waited for a cue from Keller.

Thorton yanked at her panties, and Dallas squeaked out a feeble "No."

Where the hell was her backup?

As he tried to spread her legs, Dallas instinctively kicked up both heels. She didn't have much power in this facedown position, but he felt the blow to his crotch.

"Bitch!" He slammed a hand into the back of her head. Enraged, she pushed up and rolled over.

A voice outside the vehicle shouted, "FBI! Step back and put your hands up!"

Agent Keller. Finally!

With his face only inches away, Dallas watched the rapist's expression morph from anger into confusion and fear. His hot sour breath came in rapid bursts. She put her hands against his chest and shoved. Someone grabbed him and pulled at the same time.

"Hands behind your head!" A different voice this time, bigger and louder.

More backup. The bureau probably had an agent out front too.

Thorton did as instructed. "This isn't what it looks like," he mumbled. "I was trying to help her."

Climbing from the vehicle, Dallas straightened her dress and laughed. "Oh, you helped us, all right. And we're counting on you to do more."

Chapter 25

Friday, 9:05 p.m.

Jackson and his teammates stood in the break room complaining about the crappy coffee. Schak shook his head with a "Pass," and Evans only poured herself half a cup. But Jackson filled his, dumped in cream and sugar, something he rarely did, and choked down the sludge. He needed the caffeine.

"What a shithole that place was." Evans made a face. "I feel bad for the owner. That bathroom will have to be gutted before they can rent it again."

Two fleeing occupants had been arrested, and patrol officers were still out there searching for drugs and sorting through stolen items.

"But no Bettina." Schak shook his head. "Her body will probably turn up years from now. Or she's in Guatemala."

"I think she's alive and here somewhere," Jackson countered. He used his fingers to tick off his points. "One, it's unlikely she just abandoned her mother. The autopsy report says Mrs. Rios died from a heart attack triggered by high blood sugar and dehydration, so her death was slow and painful." He glanced around but nobody had questions. "Two, Russo was traumatized by our questions about her disappearance, and he was inside her house. Why would he go there if he knew she was dead?"

"To take her panties as keepsakes." Evans touched Jackson's arm. "But I get your point. It's possible that he's keeping her captive."

A brief silence while they came to terms with the fact that they had no idea where.

"I dug into his old arrest reports," Evans said. "His mother, Melinda Russo, is listed as a third-party custody contact, but the address isn't current. Still, I'll bet he stays with her sometimes."

Many troubled young men did. Jackson met Evans' eyes. "You think Bettina might be there? Making his mother an accomplice?"

"Or a total idiot." Schak let out a harsh laugh. "There are other options."

"Like what?" A few came to mind, but Jackson wanted to know what his partner was thinking.

"Empty houses. Abandoned businesses." Schak shrugged. "A barn nobody uses."

The thought of searching every such place made them all go quiet again.

"I have a wild idea," Evans said, grinning.

A few years earlier, he would have shut her down. But not now. She used to be more unpredictable, and he was becoming less conventional. "Let's hear it."

"We let him out of jail and follow him. He might lead us right to her."

"Brilliant." Schak gave Evans' arm a friendly punch. "Since you had coffee, you can take the first shift."

Evans pivoted to Jackson. "Yes? We're going for it?"

"I have to call the DA and get him on board, but it's a valid idea."

"Unless she's dead." Schak looked sheepish. "Sorry, but I've lost all faith and optimism about everything."

Jackson couldn't argue, but he called Trang's personal cell anyway. The DA picked up right before it went to voicemail. "Hey, Jackson. What's going on?"

"I need you to call the jail and ask for Aaron Russo to be released. We want to follow him."

"Refresh my memory about who he is and why I should be involved."

Jackson gave him a rundown, stressing the urgency of the missing woman and adding, "He's charged with assaulting an officer, but that's probably just being used as leverage to get him to plead to resisting arrest."

"Fine. I'll make the call. Please don't lose him."

While waiting for the system to process Russo's release, Jackson stopped at home. Kera was in bed, reading, but his daughter wasn't there. "Has Katie been home?"

"She's working the closing shift, so she won't be here until midnight." Kera smiled sadly. "You're not staying, are you?"

He sat on the edge of the bed and kissed her. "No, sorry. I have to tail the suspect in Bettina's disappearance."

She sat up, her expression hopeful. "You think he'll lead you to her?"

"Maybe. We have to try."

"I'd love to be able to give Erica some good news."

"Me too." Jackson shifted, wanting to probe for more information. "Can you tell me if Bettina had been a surrogate before?"

Kera sighed. "I'm not sure why it matters, but no, not through our clinic."

"Thanks." He patted her leg. "I'm trying to pursue any possibility." A scenario came to mind. "What if she cheated an earlier client? Took the money and didn't deliver a baby. They might come after her for revenge. Or to steal the baby she's pregnant with."

"What a horrible thought."

Yeah, that was the business he was in. "I'm sorry. I don't mean to worry you. I'm just doing everything I can to find her."

"I appreciate that."

"I need to get back to work."

"Be safe."

Ten minutes later, he parked on a dark side street next to the jail. When inmates were released late at night—usually because of overcrowding—they went out the back door and walked along this dead-end block to reach the main street. No buses ran at this hour, so Russo would need a ride—or have to walk wherever he was going. Jackson had called the DMV earlier, and they had nothing registered in Russo's name. But that didn't mean the suspect didn't drive. If he'd kidnapped Bettina, he had to have access to a vehicle.

After twenty minutes, the wait started to annoy Jackson, and he wished he'd picked up something to eat while he was at home. He reached for the radio, then heard soft voices behind him and across the street, coming from the brick building.

Jackson scrunched down, glancing over his shoulder. Two men were walking rapidly, with a third person lagging behind. With the distance and dim lighting, he couldn't see their faces clearly. When the trio was directly across the street, he glanced over again, recognizing the third man as

Russo. Head down, he trudged along, his body languid. The other two, moving more quickly, turned toward the center of town.

At the corner, Russo headed west instead. Surprised, Jackson started his engine and cruised up to Fifth Avenue. *Where was the guy going?* He'd expected someone to be waiting with a ride, but no one stopped to pick Russo up. The suspect walked alone up the side street. Jackson hung back two blocks and stopped several times to wait, his lights off.

Eventually, Russo ended up on Railroad Boulevard, which dumped into River Road near his ex-girlfriend's neighborhood. The suspect was headed to Bettina's home again. *What the hell?* Was she captive on that property somewhere? Jackson hung back, hoping not to be spotted. At this hour, his was the only vehicle on the road. But Russo seemed oblivious.

He made the exit onto the short lane leading to the bike path and river. Jackson followed, shutting off his lights again. Past the tree-lined park entrance—where Bettina might have been abducted—Russo turned onto a side street. Jackson shut off his engine and rolled to the corner, then parked and watched. The suspect walked up to a car in a driveway of a home for sale.

Even in the dark, Jackson recognized the model, an old Mustang from the '70s. Russo pulled out a key, climbed in, and revved the engine, unconcerned about the sleeping neighbors. Jackson figured the perp had parked there before breaking into the Rios' home, then had to flee on foot. Patrol cops had apparently picked him up before he got back to his vehicle.

Jackson slumped down as Russo raced by him and out of the neighborhood. He tailed him again, less worried about being seen. The suspect sped down Chambers, not having to stop at any lights. Jackson stayed within a couple of blocks, his lights off. Russo didn't seem to notice.

They drove past Eighteenth, up Chambers, and over the hill. On the other side, the suburbs ended and the streetlights disappeared. From the top of the crest, Jackson watched the Mustang turn right onto Lorane Highway. With his lights back on now, Jackson kept following. They were outside the city limits, and the houses were infrequent. He eased off the gas, worried about being noticed. Within minutes, Russo pulled off into a driveway.

To keep his cover, Jackson drove past the exit point and turned around at an abandoned building down the road. He stopped again near the driveway, thinking this property might belong to Melinda Russo, Aaron's mother. He wanted to ask her questions anyway. Maybe now was a good time.

Should he call for backup? If Bettina was being held hostage in a shed or basement, anyone in the house might act desperately, even violently, to keep that secret. But if nothing was going on here, he didn't want to waste his team members' time. He knew his teammates were likely still awake and would want to be updated, so he texted them: *Followed Russo to 2055 Lorane Hwy. I'll keep you posted.*

Jackson slipped quietly out of the car and walked to the edge of the driveway. The house, set back from the road, looked bigger and more middle-class than the other two he'd visited on this case. He moved quickly toward it, muffling his footsteps by staying on the grass between the gravel and the trees. As Russo neared the front porch, floodlights came on and someone stepped out. Even in the unflattering glare, the woman's face was striking, but her mouth was set in a grim line. "Aaron? What are you doing here?"

"Getting closure." Russo pushed past her into the home. She hurried after him, closing the door and cutting off their voices.

Jackson stood at the edge of the circular driveway, shadowed by trees, and tried to make up his mind. Should he give up his cover so he could question the woman? Or wait and see if Russo left again? Her tone—like a mother speaking to her child—indicated he didn't really belong here. But the suspect's reference to "closure" seemed ominous.

Jackson took a few steps toward the porch and heard the distinctive sound of a door closing behind the house. Someone was in the backyard. Jackson ran along the side of the property, past what looked like a tarp-covered ATV, and into the back clearing. He stayed along the tree line and watched as Russo entered a gardener's shed.

A moment later, he came out with a shovel.

Oh hell. A sick feeling landed in Jackson's belly. He forced himself to stay still and simply observe. If Bettina was here on the property, the shovel suggested all he would find was her corpse. Might as well let Russo lead him to it.

The suspect walked over to a small garden area and began to dig.

Clink. The sound of sharp metal striking tiny rocks in the soil.

Clink. Jackson's nerves pinged like an insect hitting a bug-zapper. How long should he wait? He slipped his phone out, wondering if he could send a text without the screen light announcing his presence. He waited another minute.

A loud clunk this time. The shovel had hit something hard. Not a body.

In the distance, a car engine roared along the road, then slowed near the entrance to the property. He hoped it was

Schak or Evans.

At the sound, Russo stopped digging and spun in Jackson's direction. Time to move. He rushed forward, his hand inside his jacket, ready to pull his weapon. "Eugene Police. Put the shovel down!"

"What?" Russo dropped the tool.

"Hands in the air!" Jackson shouted.

The man complied, his face confused and contorted with pain. The back door banged open and his mother yelled, "What's happening?" A set of motion-sensor lights came on.

Jackson let go of his gun and pulled cuffs instead. The woman ran down the stone path, her slippers flapping. She stopped next to him. "Who are you?"

"Detective Jackson, EPD."

Evans suddenly jogged up, her weapon drawn.

"This is Detective Evans." Jackson stepped toward Russo. "What are you digging up?"

Russo stared down at the hole. "Memories."

Evans holstered her weapon and squatted near the dirt pile. She pulled until she freed a small box from the soil. A tiny padlock secured its secrets.

But it wasn't a body. Jackson breathed a quiet sigh of relief.

The woman grabbed her son's arm. "Is this about Bettina? I told you to let her go."

"I'm trying." The young man burst into tears.

Chapter 26

Saturday, September 21, 12:35 a.m.

After a quick trip to her hotel room to change into pants, Dallas sped back to the Vancouver bureau. Agent Keller had loaned her the car and promised to delay the interrogation until she arrived. Dallas was grateful for the opportunity to participate. Usually, once her undercover work wrapped up, the bureau sent her back to Phoenix to write reports—while the specialists extracted information from the arrested criminals.

After passing through the security measures to access the field office, the front-desk agent led her to a break room and told her to wait. Knowing she might not get back to her hotel to sleep until sometime tomorrow, Dallas brewed a cup of dark Keurig. She glanced at her phone and realized it was technically Saturday already.

As she gulped her coffee, Keller stepped into the room. "You ready?" The agent had taken off her knit cap, but was still dressed like a guy on his way to a football game.

"Always." Dallas gave a tight smile.

They zigzagged to the rear of the quiet building, not seeing anyone else. Big-city bureaus like the one in Phoenix kept several agents on duty around-the-clock, but she'd been inside a few small-town field offices that only employed a few agents.

The interrogation room was so bright Dallas blinked and wished for sunglasses. The perp sat cuffed to the table, his eyes jittery.

"I want a lawyer." He tried, and failed, to sound confident.

"I already let you make a call," Keller said. "Apparently you don't know an attorney who will come down here right now and represent you. So let's get started."

Thorton jerked his head toward Dallas. "She entrapped me."

Dallas held back a laugh and a snarky retort. She would let Keller lead, until the other agent signaled her.

"There are two known facts that you have to accept." Keller's voice sounded calm and pleasant as she looked right at Thorton. "You are going to answer questions, and you are going to prison." The agent toyed with a smile. "The only unknowns are which prison and how long."

"It's not like it seems. I wasn't really—"

"Shut up!" Suddenly angry, Keller's face contorted. "You're lucky my partner didn't break any of your bones when you assaulted her. I would have." She leaned in. "There is no more sympathy for guys like you. The only thing you can do to help yourself is to confess and cooperate fully."

"Cooperate? I kind of already did."

"Getting caught doesn't count," Keller scoffed. "How many women did you assault? By our count, it's eight, possibly nine."

An exaggeration to get him to correct it and admit to more than one.

"No. That's crazy. I've never done this before."

Keller listed all the names of the victims the bureau had tracked in the last six months.

Thorton didn't respond, but his left eye started to twitch.

Dallas cut in, unable to stop herself. "I'll bet Deanna Sharp can identify you. She remembers the attack, and a jury will sympathize with her. You'll be labeled and judged publicly as a sexual predator."

Thorton silently stared at the wall, his only movement the involuntary eye spasms.

"We need a full confession," Keller prompted.

"Why? It was only this one time, and you were both there." He'd lost his confidence.

"We still need a statement." Keller pushed a notepad across the table, then got up to uncuff him.

"You mean write it down?" He seemed confused by the request.

"Yes."

"I can't write. I mean, it's really hard for me." He flushed with embarrassment.

"We'll let you record your statement, but you have to confess to at least three assaults." This time Keller pushed a digital device across to him.

Dallas wanted to laugh again. This whole conversation was on camera.

Thorton tried not to look at the device. "Hey, I admit I tried to finger this woman." He gestured at Dallas as though she was inconsequential. "And maybe one other. But you're really blowing this up."

"We have the glass with your fingerprints and the beer with the rohypnol. I also took a video of you dumping it." Keller was deadpan. "Intentionally drugging someone is second-degree assault, and you'll spend five years in federal prison." She paused. "Just for that single count. Throw in all the sexual assaults, plus other druggings . . ." She let him do the math.

The twitch escalated into rapid blinking of both eyes.

Keller kept up the pressure. "Remember when I mentioned the various kinds of prisons? Judges take our recommendations seriously."

Tiny beads of sweat formed on his upper lip. "Can I get some water?"

"In a minute." Keller waited to see if he would start to confess.

When he didn't, she stood, so Dallas did too. They walked out.

Relieved to be in the hall where it was cooler and dimmer, Dallas asked, "What now?"

"We let him sit for twenty minutes and come back with some water. Then we hit him with what we really want."

Dallas paced for most of the break, afraid she would get sleepy if she stopped moving.

Back under the bright lights of the interrogation room, she regretted wearing a sweater. Keller held onto the bottle of water she'd brought in and stared at Thorton. "There's another option."

"What?" Eagerness revived him.

Keller glanced at Dallas.

Her turn! She leaned forward. "We need you to tell us about your online buddies."

What little color Thorton had in his face washed away. "I don't know what you're talking about."

"No Consent Needed, your criminal forum. We—"

He shouted over her. "It's not my website! I just comment there sometimes."

"You send the private invitations, so we know the score. And we want names, locations, and crimes."

"I don't know anything," he pleaded.

"That's too bad." Keller shrugged. "The only way you're getting a deal, meaning two or three years instead of fifteen, is to give us something in return."

Dallas wanted to get into details. "I'm particularly interested in *KingCock*, who said a friend had kept someone captive."

"I don't know any of them personally." Thorton sounded sincere, but desperate. "They're just online masks, and I think most of them are full of shit."

He knew something! Dallas pressed again. "Tell us about *KingCock's* friend. Is he online?" The freak had probably been talking about himself. "What do you know about *KingCock*."

"I don't know anything." A thin film of moisture had formed on his cheeks. "I don't feel well. Can I have that water?"

Keller looked at Dallas, implying it was her decision.

"Not yet. I need to know that you're done shielding your accomplices."

Thorton closed his eyes. "I really don't know anything about the others on the site."

"Except that they all hate women." Dallas decided to bring up his crimes again, just to remind him how much trouble he faced. "How many women have you assaulted? We intend to locate them all."

Thorton stared at her for a full count of ten.

She waited him out.

"Do you promise I won't get more than two years?"

A crack! Dallas knew the state's attorney general would have to make the deal, but they could give recommendations. "Only if you give us something that leads to the arrest of another criminal. That's how this works."

The perp wiped his sweaty cheeks. "There's another guy, *JungleBoy*. He lives in Eugene, and I think he might have kidnapped someone."

Chapter 27

Bettina lay awake, her mind and body humming. Other than shuffling around the room, she hadn't exercised in a week—or however long she'd been down here—and she felt pressure building inside her. She'd tried to track the time, but since Sweaty kept odd hours and stopped in to rape her in the middle of the night, she rarely slept, except superficially. Exhausted, yet jumpy, she finally sat up.

The house had been quiet for a while, and she hoped he was sleeping. He'd taken off her shackles earlier for sex and hadn't put them back. Maybe this was her only opportunity. Bettina tapped the tiny battery-powered nightlight he'd finally brought down, and the edges of everything came into view. She squatted near the end of the mattress, grabbed the seam, and pulled up with all her might. She managed to hoist the heavy thing onto her thighs. Its weight made her legs wobble. The next part would be even harder.

With her hands under the mattress, she sucked in all the oxygen her lungs could hold and heaved it up toward the wall. The mattress thumped the concrete and started to slide sideways. She leapt over the corner to catch it with her body, then muscled the mattress back into a vertical position under the window. Feeling dizzy, she bent over and breathed deeply.

159

When she felt better, she took a short run at the mattress and started to climb. It started to slide. *Damn!* She stopped and pushed the bed back into place. She needed a block of some kind. The only other thing in the room was the damaged loveseat. Adrenaline pumping, Bettina pulled it away from the other wall and dragged it a few feet toward the mattress. Out of breath again, she moved around to the back of the loveseat and pushed it the rest of the way.

Now that the mattress was wedged to the wall, she tried to climb it again, keeping her body snug against it. As she reached the top, the bed slid sideways—but only a few inches.

The window was right there. And so narrow. Could she squeeze her body through it? First she had to break it, then bust out all the glass. She pulled the nightlight from the waistband of her pants and hoped it was solid enough to do the job. She had to be fast about all of it.

Bettina slammed the plastic light into the glass as hard as she could.

The loud whack reverberated through the walls. But the glass didn't break. Heart pounding, she smashed it again. The pane cracked this time, a sharp distinctive sound. Oh god, he'd probably heard all of it.

His footsteps pounded above her, moving rapidly across the floor.

Breath ragged, she smashed the glass, breaking out a few chunks. They tumbled down the mattress. The door at the top of the stairs burst open.

"What the fuck?" His voice boomed through the room.

Bettina couldn't make herself look at him. Frantic, she bashed her fist into the last chunk of glass. It broke free and fell to the ground outside. Just as she pushed her head into the opening, her feet lost their grip and she started to slide. *No!*

Angry hands encircled her ankles and pulled her down. The man grabbed her hair and yanked her away from the mattress. "Don't make me hurt you!" He shoved her aside, threw the mattress to the floor, then knocked her onto it.

Bettina scrambled backward, trying to get away from him, but there was nowhere to go. As he reattached her shackles, pain flared in her right hand. She glanced at the cut on her knuckle, oozing with blood.

"I brought you warm water and soap!" he yelled. "And this is how you thank me?" He sounded hurt.

"I'm sorry." She had to calm him and salvage what she could. "Thank you. I'm just scared. You can understand that, can't you?"

Silently, he stared at her pubic area.

A cramp seized her lower belly. Bettina instinctively cupped the baby.

"You're bleeding."

She glanced at her hand again. "It's just a little cut."

"Not there." He shook his head and pointed between her legs. "There."

Oh no! Bettina glanced down. The mattress had a dark maroon spot. "It's nothing."

"You're holding your belly. You're pregnant."

Would he kill her now? Before she could plead for herself and her baby, the man stepped back, as if she were suddenly contaminated.

"This is a problem."

Chapter 28

Saturday, 4:45 a.m.

Sophie parked in the lot behind the printing press, trying to remember the last time she'd been up this early for work. *Never?* The drivers and carriers who delivered the paper got up in the dark every day, so she'd survive. *But this had better pay off.*

She got out and hurried over to the loading dock, where a two-man production crew stacked newspaper bundles for pickup. A few drivers were already lined up in their cars, waiting. The bundle haulers dropped off papers with carriers, who then delivered routes on foot. Some drivers also handled routes themselves, and others worked split shifts, coming back in the afternoons to deliver the marketing material the company printed for other businesses. Or at least that's how she thought it all worked. Her goal this morning was to find Sam and ask him about Carl, the homicide victim.

The drivers all had their engines idling. Sophie approached a woman in an old van who looked seventy and rather beat up. Sophie felt sorry for her, having to do this job. She tapped on the window, and the woman reluctantly rolled it down.

"Yeah?"

"I'm Sophie and I write for the paper. I cover crime and

courts." She smiled, remembering to be charming, even though it was dark, cold, and god-awful early.

"And?"

"I'm looking for a bundle hauler named Sam. Can you point him out?"

"He's not here yet. Which is a little odd. He's usually first in line."

"What does he drive?"

"A brown truck. Why? What do you want with him?" She stiffened, a little defensive.

Did the drivers look out for each other? Like a family? That might be a good freelance piece. Sophie refocused on her mission. "I'm actually curious about a guy named Carl who worked here as a carrier last summer. He was murdered recently, and I want to know more about him. To humanize his story, so he's not just another crime statistic."

"That's a shame." Her tone didn't convey any real feeling.

Sophie shivered in the chill, suddenly feeling like she was wasting her time. "Anyway, I heard that Sam was friendly with him."

The old woman laughed. "They're brothers. So yeah, they were friendly."

A detail for her story. Now she really wanted to find Sam Turnbull. "They have different last names, so Jeanie didn't seem to know they were related."

"That was on purpose. Sam didn't want to lose his job if Carl messed up or got fired."

"Carl was a screw-up?"

"A recovering addict, so yeah."

Sophie pulled out her yellow tablet and made notes. "Do you know anything else about him?"

"Sam mentioned growing up in Costa Rica."

Interesting. Carl's photo didn't suggest he was Hispanic. "They're immigrants?"

"Uh, I don't think so. They seem American."

Whatever that meant. "Can I get your name?"

"No. You can't quote me in the paper. I don't want to lose my job." The old woman started to roll up her window.

"Wait!" Sophie put her hand on the glass. "I won't use your name, I promise. I'm just trying to be friendly."

A slight hesitation. "Sally."

"Thanks, Sally. Do you know how to contact Sam?"

She laughed again. "We chatted a few times, but we didn't sub for each other. This bunch of misfits out here"—she gestured at the vehicles lined up behind her—"are not exactly the social type."

"Who did sub for Sam?"

"No one. He never missed a shift that I know of." Looking over her shoulder, she searched the bundle-hauler line. "Which is why I can't believe he didn't show up this morning." She started to roll the window again, then stopped. "But hey, he might be here this afternoon for the commercial bundles."

"What time?"

"Two. Gotta go, the papers are ready." She rolled forward as she talked.

Sophie stepped back and watched as the old woman loaded bundles off the dock and into her van. She hoped like hell she wouldn't have to work that hard when she was old.

Chapter 29

Saturday, 8:25 a.m.

Jackson entered the conference room, carrying a box of goodies he'd picked up at Voodoo Doughnuts. A task force meeting this early on Saturday called for some kind of treat. He should have stopped at Full City to get coffee too, but he'd already hit his limit on caffeine for the morning and was running late. He hadn't gone to sleep until two, and the boys had bolted out of bed at five-thirty to build a living-room fort with boxes and blankets. Jackson had finished a pot of java by six.

He missed slow-moving weekends with Katie, welding and chatting in the garage. He never went fishing with Schak anymore either. Jackson hardly recognized his life now. But this—sitting here in the conference room, analyzing details and formulating theories—was consistent and familiar. So he was glad to be here.

Evans hurried in behind him. "Good morning." She grinned, her eyes glinting brightly. Was she taking that prescription again? The one that kept her sharp and alert even without sleep? *Damn,* he needed to get some. But the effort would require seeing a doctor and asking for the drug—admitting vulnerability—so it would never happen.

"Morning. Thanks again for showing up last night."

"Wouldn't have missed it." She sat and reached for a doughnut. "I skipped breakfast because I knew you would bring these. Your guilt is so predictable." She smiled again, patting his arm.

Schak sauntered in, sat across from Evans, and glanced back and forth at them. "How'd it go last night?" Schak had called, asking if Jackson needed him, but by that point he didn't. "The suspect's mother, Melinda Russo, let us search her house. Unless she has a secret room we couldn't find, Bettina wasn't there."

"We should check the blueprints on file with the county just in case." Schak reached for a doughnut, scowling. "No maple and bacon?"

Jackson ignored him. "The property office won't open again until Monday, but I assume you'll be first in line to get those specs."

Schak grunted.

Evans chuckled, then added, "Russo went out there to dig up a box of keepsakes." She gestured at Jackson. "Show him."

Jackson pulled a large evidence bag from his satchel. He planned to drop it at the crime lab after the meeting. The ornate bronze box showed through the clear plastic, so Jackson didn't bother to pull it out. Dirt still clung to the sides. "It contains a lock of Bettina's hair, a ticket stub, and a pair of panties. Russo says he buried the keepsakes when Bettina broke up with him."

Schak raised an eyebrow. "He's locked up again, correct?"

"Yes, but the charge is still *assaulting an officer*. It's not a crime to be weirdly sentimental."

"He's freaking creepy." Evans made a wild-eyed expression.

"Why did he dig them up?" Schak asked.

"He says he wanted to give them back now that his heart tells him Bettina's dead." Jackson didn't know what to think about Russo, except that the guy likely had mental health problems.

"I still think he knows where Bettina is," Evans insisted. "We need a warrant to dig up that whole backyard."

Jackson concurred but didn't think a judge would see it their way. "I ran a background on Melinda Russo, and she's squeaky clean except for a possession charge twenty-five years ago."

"She could still be an accomplice," Schak countered.

"She let us search her house." Evans glanced at Schak, who had frosting on his upper lip. "But I get your point. I know police officers have searched homes, then had to go back with sledgehammers to find kids in secret rooms or bodies in the basement."

A queasy feeling hit Jackson's gut. Had they made a mistake? "You can certainly write up a warrant and ask a judge to sign it. I'll go back with you and search again, if you get permission."

"I'm on it." Evans gave a tight smile.

It would be a waste of time. They didn't have enough evidence to suggest Aaron Russo had harmed his ex-girlfriend. They needed to place him at the scene during the time she went missing. Jackson remembered Karen Silas' comment. "Bettina's neighbor says she saw Russo on Saturday not far from where he left his car. Let's pin her down on the time and get a signed statement for the judge." Jackson spoke to Schak. "Any luck with financial and phone records?"

"Nope. There were no bank documents in her house. So she either doesn't have an account or does all her banking electronically. Without her phone or computer, I have no way to track any of it." He held up a hand. "But her mother had cell service through Sprint, so I requested records for both of them. Those docs have not arrived yet."

"What about medical?" Evans stared hard at Jackson. "Can you get access to her records from the fertility clinic?"

"I asked. Kera says there's nothing in her file that would help us." He let out a long breath. "I'm out of ideas. Do either of you have one?"

A moment of silence.

"We could offer a reward." Evans didn't sound optimistic.

"That's a good way to waste time with a bunch of crackpots," Schak complained. "If the public was going to help us with her, they would have already."

"I want to take another run at interrogating Russo," Jackson said. "We'll give him another night in jail, then maybe offer a plea deal that allows him to spend his life in a psychiatric hospital instead of prison."

Schak scoffed. "The DA will never go for it."

"You're probably right." Jackson hated giving up, but they still had to locate her body. The mother of the baby she'd been carrying needed closure, a chance to grieve and move on. In addition, Bettina and her mother probably had family members in Guatemala who needed to be informed.

They were all quiet for a moment, his teammates likely thinking the same thing.

Schak broke the silence. "What's the update with our dead guy?"

Relieved to change the subject, Jackson perked up. "His name is Carl Jagger, and he worked as a carrier for the *Willamette News* briefly last summer. But we can't find any family members or social media profiles. He was a loner."

"A drug mule," Schak muttered. "Isn't that what the autopsy revealed?"

"Most likely. But he was killed in our jurisdiction, so we're not giving up on him yet either." Jackson remembered his latest effort to track Carl. "I called his previous landlord, but he hasn't gotten back to me yet." Jackson pulled out his phone and tried again. No point in waiting.

The landlord answered. "Randy Stoops here." He had a pleasant but no-nonsense voice.

"Detective Jackson. I called earlier about a rental that was occupied by Carl Jagger. I need his forwarding address if you have it."

"Sure. I meant to call you." Papers rustled in the background. "I have no idea if it's still current, but I can tell you where I sent his refund check."

A drug addict had gotten his deposit back? "I'm ready." Jackson reached for a pen.

The property owner rattled off a long number on Willow Creek. As Jackson repeated it back, he noticed Evans keying the address into her tablet. "Anything else you can tell me about your tenant?"

"Sorry, but I really don't remember. I have dozens of rentals."

Jackson thanked him and ended the call. He looked up at his teammates. "I have a feeling this trip will be pointless, but I'll head out there anyway."

"Want me to go with you?" Evans asked. "The location isn't too far from the old Hynix plant."

"Thanks, but you have to write a subpoena." He focused on Schak. "And you need to put down that third doughnut."

Chapter 30

Just before Eighteenth Avenue dead-ended into the abandoned computer-chip factory, Jackson took a left on Willow Creek. The rural road wandered past wetlands, ponds, and clusters of oaks. He drove slowly, watching for addresses on mailboxes. He eventually spotted the matching numbers on a post near an alder tree and pulled down the dirt drive. The home, about five-hundred yards back, was a strange construction mix. The original structure, not much more than a shack, had been added onto with no attempt to blend the siding or roof material. A freestanding carport looked like it had been built without the benefit of safety codes.

No dogs barked or charged his car, so Jackson considered that a good sign—unless Carl Jagger's pets had died of neglect or wandered off after their owner was killed. If the dead man had been a drug runner, he'd likely lived entanglement free.

Was that his truck under the carport? Jackson walked toward the weathered door, but before he reached it a man stepped out. Mid-to-late twenties, five-nine, and blond scraggly hair. "What can I do for you?" He kept his mouth tight as he talked, but the decay on his teeth showed through anyway and his breath smelled like cigarettes.

"Detective Jackson, Eugene Police. I'm looking for Carl

Jagger's next of kin."

The man's face froze—then crumbled. He reached up with both hands and rubbed vigorously, maybe trying to distract himself.

"What's your name?"

"Sam Turnbull." He spoke softly.

"Are you related to Carl?"

"His brother."

Oh yeah. The Lucky Clover bartender had mentioned a brother, but that seemed like weeks ago. "I'm sorry, but I have bad news."

Sam nodded. "What this time?" Tears started to pool in his eyes.

"He's dead, and I need your help finding who killed him. Can I come in?"

The brother didn't move, just stood, quietly crying.

Jackson gave him a minute. "I know you're grieving, but I have to ask questions."

No response.

"When did you last see Carl?"

Sam brought his hands together and pinched the tender skin in the pocket of his thumb.

Physical pain to control his emotional pain?

After a moment, he said, "Maybe a month ago. Carl relapsed again and has been using. Maybe dealing too. I want no part of it, so I haven't been in touch with him."

That supported their suspicions. "Did Carl have a girlfriend?"

"Not recently."

"Do you know who would want to kill him?"

"No, but if he's involved with drugs . . ."

No need to finish the thought. Except Jackson needed

information. "Do you know the names of his friends? Or connections?"

Sam paused to think. "He mentioned someone named Chase once. They hung out at a tavern near Four Corners."

They were back to Chase Cortez, who'd made bail and gone underground. Frustrated, Jackson pressed the grieving brother. "Where did Carl live?"

"Maybe he stayed with Chase. I don't know. I kicked him out months ago." Sam's eyes flashed with guilt and anger. "Because of the heroin." He pushed a hand through his tangled hair, and his sleeve pulled back, revealing a round purple scar on his forearm.

The brothers were a mystery with their different last names and contrasting appearances, but they shared *some* things. "Tell me about the scars. Carl had them too."

Sam's jaw tightened, the muscles twitching. "Just staph-infected bug bites from long ago." He grunted. "And a treatment that was worse than the problem."

"Costa Rica?"

His eyes went wary. "What do you know about that?"

"Nothing, except that Carl mentioned it to someone in the tavern." Jackson shifted, eager to see the house. "Can we go inside and talk?"

Sam stiffened and stepped back. "What else is there to say?"

Quite a bit, in fact. Time to ask the most important question. "What were you doing Tuesday night, around seven?"

"Why? Is that when Carl died?" Sam's eyes hardened, a coldness creeping in.

The geography suddenly mapped out in Jackson's mind. "His body was found over this hill on the corner of Crow and

Highway 126." Jackson pointed in the general direction, just to get his own bearings.

"Huh. Like I said, I haven't seen him." The brother seemed detached now.

"Do you own a gun?"

"No."

Had he responded too quickly? Jackson searched Sam's face for signs of lying. But the man was a mask.

He seemed to be done talking. "Do I need to claim Carl's body or something?"

"Yes. You also have to arrange for him to be transferred to a funeral home."

"I can't afford nothing like that." The brother stepped back and reached behind for the doorknob. "Sorry, but I have stuff to do." He pivoted, pushed open the door, and disappeared behind it with the distinctive click of a deadbolt.

If not for the proximity to where the gunshot victim had been dumped, Jackson might have walked away without much follow-up. But these guys were too odd to ignore, and he needed a strategic approach. As he left, Jackson took the long route—just in case Sam Turnbull kept a roll of black plastic stashed somewhere. As Jackson rounded the carport, he glanced over his shoulder at the far side of the house. A living room window near the front and something narrow and low to the ground in the back. A vent? He couldn't tell from this distance.

Walking slowly, he passed the truck, glancing in the back for bloodstains or pieces of plastic. The cargo area was scratched and dented, but clean, like it had been recently hosed out.

Chapter 31

Jackson drove away, feeling uneasy. He suspected Sam Turnbull knew more than he was telling. He may not have killed his brother himself, but he could have been involved somehow, or knew who'd done it and why. Maybe they were both drug runners and Carl's addiction had become a liability.

Sam could just be a grieving brother with a clean truck. His distress had seemed real, at least at first. Now that Jackson had notified the family, he felt less pressure to work overtime investigating the homicide. The case could stay on the back burner—until they found the missing woman. Bettina was more important. He didn't feel optimistic about solving Carl's murder in the traditional short-term way. More likely, the truth would come out over time as they arrested the people involved for other crimes and they ratted each other out to get plea bargains for themselves.

Back at his desk, Jackson ran Turnbull through the database. Nothing came up, so he called a friend at the DMV. "Hey, it's Jackson. Will you run a name for me?"

"Sure. There's only a hundred people in the lobby." Sarcasm was Stacy's operating mode.

"A typical day for your crew." Jackson gave her the name. "This shouldn't take long. Please and thank you."

"Hang on." Canned pop music filled his ear. He glanced through his to-do list, noting that he had several more calls to make. Stacy came back on. "Sam Turnbull owns a 2004 Chevy truck, listed as brown. You want the plate number?"

He'd memorized it when he was there, but took the information anyway, in case the vehicle was stolen. The numbers matched. "How long has he owned it?"

"Since May of last year."

"What about Carl Jagger?"

Stacy sighed. "Spelled with a C or K?"

"C."

When she got back to him, she spoke quickly. "Silver, 1998 Toyota Corolla, with an expired registration. I have to go." She was gone before he could thank her. Jackson made a mental note to send her some chocolate.

So where was Carl's car?

Had the killers dumped it somewhere? Maybe the ancient vehicle had been melted into scrap long ago. Yet if Carl had been making trips across the border with narcotics, he'd likely driven. Possibly the dealer/perp had kept the car and passed it over to his next mule.

An image popped into his head. He knew where he'd seen the car! Bettina Rios' driveway. After finding her mother's dead body, he'd asked forensic technicians to transport it to the evidence bay to be searched and fingerprinted.

Well, crap. Did that mean Bettina was a drug carrier too? Would they eventually find her body wrapped in plastic and dumped in the woods? Jackson called Joe at the crime lab and left a message: "I need to know everything about the car found at the Rios home. ASAP." He stood and grabbed his jacket. Time to talk to the ex-boyfriend again.

Jackson trudged up the long staircase at the jail, aware that nothing hurt this time. The relief wouldn't last, but he was grateful for it.

As he entered the lobby, the desk deputy abruptly stood and spoke to an older deputy behind her, then made an announcement over the speaker system. "Our lobby and front desk are temporarily closed. Everybody needs to leave."

Something intense was going down. In a building full of criminals, you could count on that regularly. Jackson glanced around. Only two people sat on the bench against the wall, a skinny middle-aged woman trying to look twenty and a grandma-type who didn't care about her appearance. They both looked upset, but didn't complain or ask questions. They'd obviously dealt with the whims and inconsistencies of the county jail before.

He strode up to the plexiglass-enclosed counter. "Detective Jackson, EPD. What's going on?" He didn't really want to know, but to get inside and see his suspect, he had to work with their circumstances.

"We've had a suicide," the deputy said, her voice tight. "Now is not a good time."

"I understand. But I'm trying to find a missing woman, so time is essential for me right now too. I need to question Aaron Russo."

Her eyes flashed with concern. "Why?"

"He may have kidnapped her, and he's the only lead we have."

She looked around, but the other deputy had left. "I'm sorry, but Aaron Russo just killed himself."

Chapter 32

Saturday, 1:25 p.m.

Sophie pushed aside her empty salad bowl, eager to get back to work. She'd spent half her morning in a stupid staff meeting with the new corporate/owner boss, then finished a follow-up story about the woman who'd been abducted at Target.

A call to the department's spokesperson had added a twist to the case. The victim had been located and "was not cooperating" with the police. That could only mean one thing—she knew the men who'd kidnapped her. Was she protecting them because they were friends or family? Or was she afraid of retaliation? Sophie realized those scenarios weren't mutually exclusive.

For now, she'd turned in her copy and wanted to get back to the mystery brothers from Costa Rica. After twenty minutes of searching online, she found an old article in a small-town newspaper near the Panamanian border. The headline read *Vegan Hippie Mom Denies Kids Antibiotics*. The photo of the child made her gasp. The little boy's face had been partially hidden by an ID-blocking bar, but his bare arms and legs were covered with the nastiest infection she'd ever seen.

Sophie skimmed through the story, absorbing the details.

An American woman named Zona Turnbull had refused to get her staph-infected children treated with antibiotics. Neighbors had taken the picture and reported her to children's services, but when caseworkers tried to intervene, the family went into hiding. *Were those kids Carl Jagger and Sam Turnbull?*

Sophie glanced at the time. *Damn.* She wanted to learn more, but she needed to get out to the loading dock right now if she hoped to talk to Sam in person.

Only a few vehicles were lined up this time, waiting for bundles—but no brown truck. Considering that his brother had just been murdered, it made sense that Sam might take time off. She would wait a while, enjoy a break in the warm fall sunshine, then go ask Jeanie for his contact information. Should she try to chat up one of the other bundle haulers instead? The old woman had indicated they weren't social people. So much for her carriers-as-a-family story.

A moment later, the van from this morning pulled up. She hurried to the end of the line, hoping Sally would chat with her again. The woman rolled her eyes as Sophie approached, but her window was open and she was smoking.

"Hey, Sally. How are you?"

"Same as this morning. And there's nothing else I can tell you about Sam."

Sophie found her curious. In fact, the whole world out here behind the printing press was mostly new to her. She'd never really thought much about the people who delivered the stories she wrote. "Can I ask why you do this? I mean, rather than a different job for income?"

"Short hours, decent pay, and very little human interaction." Sally blew smoke. "Until you came along."

Sophie laughed. "Sorry to bother you." She turned to

leave and spotted Hoogstad coming across the parking lot. "What's he doing?" She hadn't meant to say it out loud.

But Sally answered anyway. "Buying a cigarette. He claims he only allows himself two a day. So he buys them one at a time from the bundle haulers."

Huh. It was an odd method of moderation, but whatever worked for him. Sophie thanked Sally, waved at her boss, and hurried toward the production office.

After trying and failing to get Sam's contact information from Jeanie, Sophie went back to her desk and made a list for the afternoon: process her photos, get her timesheet signed, and call Jackson again. Maybe he didn't know his murder victim had a brother. She could use that info as leverage to learn more about the women's kidnapping cases, especially the one in the Target parking lot. Something really freaky was going on there.

Chapter 33

Saturday, 2:15 p.m.

Jackson sat in his sedan in the jail's parking lot and texted his teammates with the news of Russo's death. He hadn't died easily, but he had been determined. According to the in-house doctor, the inmate had stabbed himself in the jugular with a sharpened pencil, causing damage and bleeding. When that hadn't done the job fast enough, he'd wrapped a plastic trashcan liner around his neck and hung himself from the top bunk. In between those acts, Russo left a crude note, written in blood, on the concrete floor: *Sorry, Bettina!*

A confession? Jackson couldn't tell. Why the hell hadn't the bastard told them where to find the poor woman's body? A goddamn apology didn't do her or her family any good.

Rage building—both at Russo and the jail personnel for letting it happen—Jackson struggled with what to do next. He remembered that Bettina's car needed to be checked out and that he should confer with his team about Sam Turnbull. He sent Schak and Evans a second text: *Let's meet for dinner at 5 at McMenamins.* That gave him a few hours to make some progress.

He cut over to Second Avenue, drove out to Garfield, and arrived at the crime lab in six minutes. As he pulled into the boxy gray-brick building with no windows or signs, his phone rang. Sophie Speranza again. He might as well get this over with. "Hello, Sophie."

"Hey, Jackson. I hope this means you're finally going to give me an update on the gunshot victim."

He couldn't recall what he'd already told her and figured he had nothing to lose. "His name is Carl Jagger, with a C. He lived in Costa Rica for a while and moved here with his brother." Jackson held back the name. He didn't want to spook the guy.

"You know about Sam?"

How did she? "I just met him this morning. How do you know his name?"

"He's a bundle hauler for the newspaper."

Why the hell hadn't the production lady told him that? "Uh, thanks. Good to know."

"Any idea who shot Carl? Or why?"

"Not yet." Jackson decided to share his theory. "He may have been a drug runner." Making that info public might prompt a witness to come forward.

"You think Carl was transporting narcotics between here and Costa Rica?" Excitement sparked in her voice now.

"It's just a working theory. We don't have anything else."

A moment of quiet, except for the computer clicks in the background. "He doesn't have an online presence," Sophie mused.

"I know. I have to get back to work." Jackson started to end the call.

"What about the missing woman? Bettina Rios, I mean. Any leads on her?"

"No. But we could use another public prompt."

"What about the other woman, Sarvis Martin, who was kidnapped in the Target parking lot?"

Jackson sighed. He'd heard a few details, but the case was still in the hands of patrol officers. "She's fine, but refuses to cooperate. That's all I know."

"She looks a lot like Bettina. Is there a connection? Is someone targeting a specific type of woman?"

He briefly wondered the same thing but didn't have enough information yet.

When he didn't respond, Sophie kept going. "Is her abduction about drugs? Did she rip off a dealer?"

Jackson's head pounded. Too many unanswered questions and not enough sleep. "I really don't know. It's not my case." He prayed it wouldn't be. But what if all these crimes were part of a narcotic smuggling operation that was experiencing an internal fracture?

"I have to tell our readers something," Sophie pleaded.

Jackson decided to give her information that would soon be public anyway. "Bettina's ex-boyfriend, Aaron Russo, just committed suicide in jail. His final message was an apology to Bettina." Jackson felt his throat closing up. "So we're likely looking for her body."

Unable to say more, he ended the call.

A wave of depression hit him hard. So many men were troubled and violent. They left a trail of destruction everywhere they went and hurt everyone they came in contact with. The shame they brought to his gender disgusted him. Nothing he did on the job ever changed that. He didn't know if he could continue. Seeing the darkest side of human nature was slowly robbing him of his ability to feel joy. It wasn't fair to Kera and the boys either. Something had to change.

Maybe he would see a counselor. The department had several on staff, and the sessions were kept confidential. He couldn't think about that right now. Jackson waved his security card in front of the little camera, and the gate lifted, letting him drive to the back parking lot.

As he climbed out, his phone beeped. A text from Sophie: *Not sure if it's important, but forgot to tell you that Sam didn't show up for work today.*

Jackson stopped to think about it. The guy had just learned this morning that his brother was dead. According to Sophie, Sam was a newspaper carrier and that meant his job started quite early. Jackson hadn't shown up to notify him until after nine. Had Sam already missed his shift? Did it matter? People skipped work all the time for any number of reasons. Jackson set the issue aside for later. Right now, he had a missing woman's car to check out.

Chapter 34

Saturday, 3:00 p.m.

Dallas woke to her phone alarm and sat up. *Where the hell—?*

The hotel room came into focus. A moment later, her brain did too. *Oh right.* Vancouver. Undercover. Bringing down a ring of sexual predators. She bolted out of bed and splashed cold water on her face. Two hours of sleep in the middle of the day could feel worse than no rest at all, but only for the ten minutes right after she woke up. She brewed a cup of coffee, added cream to cool it off, then downed it like a life-saving medicine. She had a flight to catch in a few hours. In the meantime, she had to learn everything she could about *JungleBoy.*

Forty minutes later, she gave up. Other than his presence in the incel conversations, he didn't exist online. At least not in any form connected to that persona. She hoped the bureau techs would have better luck tracking his location. Dallas made herself a second cup, then sat back and savored it, staring out the window. There had to be a way to find him.

What if she could get him to tell her? Excitedly brainstorming ideas, Dallas logged into the No Consent forum and scrolled through recent threads, landing on one about women's hygiene. The content was bizarre, disgusting, and painfully ignorant. After a few minutes, she found a comment *JungleBoy* had posted that morning: *My girl wants to wash down there but its to late. I think Im gonna trade her in.*

What the hell did that mean? "My girl" sounded possessive, as though he had already taken someone captive, and "trade her in" sounded ominous, implying another woman could be in danger. Posting as *bi*chgirlhater,* Dallas responded: *Ill take her if your done. I dont mind used goods. Pussy is pussy. <grin>*

Nervous that she'd blown it by sounding too eager, Dallas paced the room. Maybe she shouldn't have been so direct. But he might not see her comment for days, if ever. The website wasn't Facebook. It didn't notify users when someone responded to a post—and she didn't have time to waste. She finished her last-minute packing and took a cab to the airport.

While waiting to board her flight, she checked the website again and found a response from *JungleBoy*: *Only if you let me watch! <snicker>*

Yes! He had engaged. She quickly keyed in a retort: *Name the time & place. I'll bring beer & condoms.* Dallas changed her mind and corrected the last part to *beer & hard cock.* She hit the return key to post it and looked at the people in the boarding line. The final segment hadn't moved. Dallas clicked over to the main Not Normal site just to kill a few minutes. No posts from *JungleBoy* there. She tabbed back to the No Consent thread, but he hadn't commented again.

Dallas read through a few more conversations, shaking her head and looking forward to never seeing this slimy stuff again. In the background, she heard the airline calling a passenger. *Some idiot was about to miss her flight.* She read a few more comments.

"Amber Davison, please report to Gate B-36. Your flight has boarded."

Oh shit! That was her. Dallas slammed her laptop closed and hustled over to a gate marked Eugene. She hoped Brett Thorton hadn't given her a phony lead just to buy himself time.

Chapter 35

Saturday, 3:05 p.m.

Inside the crime lab, Jackson hurried upstairs. Jasmine Parker, who'd just been promoted to head the crime lab, stepped out of her office as he entered the hall. "Hey, Parker. How's the new position?"

"You already know. Too much to do and not enough money to hire anyone."

"I feel that. Is Joe around? I'm looking for updates."

"He's in the big bay."

Jackson nodded and jogged back downstairs. The two processing bays looked like garages, only brighter and cleaner. He found the technician in the front seat of Bettina Rios' vehicle.

"Hey, Joe."

The stout man jerked up in surprise and banged his head on the interior roof.

"Sorry. I didn't mean to startle you."

"I'm fine." He rubbed his head as he climbed out.

Jackson stayed focused. "Did you find anything worth noting?"

"No blood, if that's what you're asking." Joe pulled off his latex gloves. "I haven't taken any prints yet, because nobody indicated this was a crime scene, and I don't have a profile to compare them to. But I will if necessary."

Jackson tried to articulate what he wanted from the vehicle. "I just need to determine if the abductor was in the car or left something that would help identify him." Even if they found something of Russo's, it might only mean he'd ridden with Bettina when they were dating. But if they found another suspect and could match his prints, that changed everything. Not likely though. Russo had pretty much confessed. He still didn't have a proper crime scene for either of his cases. Jackson felt his body tense.

"You look annoyed." Joe cocked his head.

"I'm not upset with you. Our only suspect in Bettina's abduction just committed suicide in jail, and I'm worried we'll never know what happened to this poor woman."

"Sorry, man. But I've got something that might be significant." Joe walked to the back and opened the trunk. "There's a compartment in here with traces of heroin."

Another drug angle.

Jackson stepped around the bumper for a look. Joe leaned in and pressed open a side pocket. "But it's only a trace, and I have no way of knowing how long it's been there."

Jackson couldn't help but think Bettina had been involved in the drug trade too. Maybe Russo had gotten her into it and that was why he was sorry. Or did she know Carl? They were both from Central America and had arrived in Eugene in the last few years. Maybe she'd only bought the car from him.

Oh hell! He'd forgotten to ask Stacy at the DMV for the plate number of Carl Jagger's car. It might not be the same one. Millions of these little Toyotas were on the road. Mixed emotions rolled over Jackson. Relief at having a lead to follow, yet dread for the additional work that could be involved—likely all for nothing.

Joe cut into his thoughts. "I found a couple pieces of trash under the seat too."

"Show me."

Joe handed him a small plastic tray containing a gum wrapper, a faded receipt, and a kernel of popcorn. The print on the receipt was illegible.

"And this," the technician added.

Jackson reached out to take the evidence bag. The clear plastic revealed another clear plastic bag inside, a two-inch ziplock, commonly used for drugs. "Have you analyzed the trace contents?"

"Not yet." Joe reached to take it back. "I found it wedged under the seat bracket. Again, it could have been there for a very long time."

Jackson remembered that Bettina was pregnant . . . a surrogate. Had the fertility clinic tested or screened her in any way? "Thanks, Joe. I'll get out of your way." He started to leave, then remembered the keepsakes Aaron had buried. Jackson pulled the evidence from his satchel and handed it to Joe. "Look for blood or trace evidence. If you find any, send it to the medical examiner." Jackson would have to ask Gunderson to compare it to Aaron Russo's body as well as the DNA they'd collected from Bettina's bathroom.

"I'll try to find time." Joe sounded tired.

Feeling weary himself, Jackson trudged back to his car and called Kera.

She answered with a hurried tone. "Is this important? If not, I'll call you back in ten."

"Just a quick question. Does the clinic drug test the surrogates you work with?"

"Yes, initially. Why? Do you think Bettina Rios was using?"

"Maybe. Do you check for citizenship?" He'd meant to ask

her days ago.

Kera hesitated. "We request to see two pieces of ID, one with a photo. We've never had an issue."

"Thanks. I hope none of this information turns out to be important."

"Will I see you this evening?"

"I hope to be there for dinner."

"I'd like that. Love you."

"Love you too. Bye." A sadness crept over him as he started the car and drove out. He didn't understand it, but he also didn't have time to focus on it.

As he drove toward the department, he couldn't get vehicles off his mind. Besides the silver Toyota, there was Sam's truck, which had just been washed, and Aaron's Mustang. Checking that car for blood suddenly seemed critical. He would get a towing company to haul it into the bay for examination.

Jackson's cell phone rang. *Lammers.* His gut cringed. This wouldn't be good. He pulled off the road and took the call. "Hey, boss. What's up?"

"Good news. Someone found a silver Toyota in a marsh off Pine Grove this morning." She made a displeased sound in her throat. "It took a while for the information to filter through the system, but it was registered to your victim, Carl Jagger."

Jackson breathed a sigh of relief. Maybe this was the break they needed. "Text me a GPS location, and I'll head straight out."

The rural area was southwest about four miles. Jackson texted his team to update them—and cancel their dinner plans—but requested they remain on standby. As he drove out of town, he had a sense of déjà vu. Everything connected to Carl and Sam took him in the same general direction. He hadn't asked his team to join him because this probably wasn't a crime scene. Even if Carl had been shot inside the car, which seemed unlikely, the location was obviously a dumpsite. Most of the detailed examination would be done by a forensic technician in the crime-scene bay, just as Bettina's car had been. Still, Jackson needed to see the situation for himself and do a quick interior search—if it hadn't been stripped.

The sun had dropped halfway to the horizon, but the purple and orange sky failed to hold his attention. He barely noticed the other cars on the road. Too many scenarios ran through his mind. The killer could have dumped the vehicle as an afterthought once he'd gotten rid of the body. Or he could have deliberately separated the victim from his car to make him harder to identify. Or Carl could have abandoned the old vehicle himself long ago, rather than pay a junkyard fee.

He passed through the intersection where Carl's body had been found and wondered about the woman who'd accidentally run over him. Jackson made a mental note to get in touch with her. She'd probably appreciate a follow-up.

Ten minutes and a few turns later, his GPS system informed him that the "destination was on the right." Jackson looked down the road and saw a tow truck on the edge. He parked in time to watch the tow driver descended the slope to where the little car had plunged into a cluster of tall grass and stunted willow trees. The driver secured a cable hook to the bumper and signaled his helper to start the motorized winch. The steel cable slowly pulled the battered vehicle up the embankment, making a whirring/grinding noise that was strangely satisfying.

When the Toyota was safely on the asphalt, Jackson retrieved road flags from his trunk and set them out to alert whatever traffic might buzz by. If he stayed long enough, he would need to light a couple of flares as well. As he worked, he called out to the truck driver, "I need ten minutes in the vehicle before you tow it."

The car's interior stank, and Jackson struggled to identify the sour odor. Sweat? Spilled milk? Working quickly, he picked up empty soda cans from the front floor, testing the weight to see if they were fake drug containers. None seemed to be. He searched the console next, but it contained only the usual assortment: flashlight, band-aids, half a pack of Marlboros, a pocketknife, and a registration slip. Jackson pocketed the paperwork and left the rest for Joe to tag and bag.

He shifted to the backseat where the floor was covered with an assortment of damp, dirty fast-food wrappers. So far, nothing personal and no blood that he could see or smell.

Now that he had better access, Jackson shoved his hand under the driver's seat and hit something small and solid. *A phone!* He yanked it out, optimism surging. *Please let it be Carl's. And please let it be unlocked.*

Chapter 36

Stomach growling, Jackson sat at his desk and opened a search warrant template. Sam Turnbull had lied to him. He'd claimed he hadn't heard from his brother in weeks, yet Carl's last text had been to Sam the day before he died. The message was short and simple: *What up? U want to hang? Fish?*

Sam hadn't responded.

What if Carl had gone out to his brother's anyway—and something had gone terribly wrong? They needed to get inside the house to find out for sure. Jackson's gut told him Sam would never let them in voluntarily or answer the door again. Even picking him up for questioning might require the time and patience to catch him outside his safe zone. Jackson wanted to cut through all the bullshit and get legal permission to search.

Finding a judge on a Saturday evening would be challenging, and there was no guarantee he or she would actually sign the warrant. Judges often sent law enforcement officers back to narrow the scope of the search. He planned to take it to Cranston, who tended to be more lenient than the others.

First he had to make his case. As Jackson typed out his evidentiary argument, the skimpiness of his claim became obvious. Still, he had to try. The hinky hairs on the back of his neck had been prickling since he'd left Sam's rural home that morning. The clean truck bed, missing his morning paper route, and now the blatant lie about not hearing from his brother.

Was it enough for a warrant? Especially tonight while the judge was at home. If he waited to see Cranston in his office Monday morning, he might be more amenable. But in the meantime, Sam could be bleaching his bloodstained floor. Or packing to leave town. The brothers didn't seem to have roots in Eugene, so Sam might be on the road already. Jackson quickly filled out a second warrant, asking only for the suspect's phone records, which they could use to track his movements the night of the murder. Assuming he carried his phone everywhere he went. Who didn't?

The trip to Cranston's house felt familiar. As he drove up Chambers again, Jackson put in his earpiece and used voice commands to call his daughter, worried that he hadn't heard from her since their disturbing lunch conversation. Katie didn't answer. He left her a message ending with, "Please call."

At a stoplight with no traffic, he tried Kera, who didn't pick up until the fifth ring. "Jackson. We missed you at dinner. I'm about to put the kids to bed. Are you on your way?"

"No, I'm sorry. We have a new lead in the case, and I'm trying to get a search warrant signed."

She was quiet for a moment. "I'm glad you caught a break."

She didn't say "must be nice," but he heard it anyway. "I'll spend time with the boys soon, I promise. Then you can take a long weekend afternoon with friends."

"I'll hold you to that." A pause. "Be safe."

"Always." Jackson put his phone away, a sense of guilt hovering over him. Was he taking advantage of Kera? *Only at times*, he told himself. His job wasn't always this intense, but his overtime hours had been steadily increasing for years.

Judge Cranston lived in a cul-de-sac of new homes near the peak of the hill. The two-story house boasted columns out front and a circular driveway, looking like a pretentious mini-mansion. On the walk up to the tall double doors, the scent of hot baked cheese and bread filled his nostrils. *Damn*, he was hungry. The judge would hate being interrupted at this hour.

A soft-spoken woman in an apron answered the door. "You're here to see my husband, aren't you?"

"Yes, ma'am." Jackson tried to smile, but the tension in his jaw wouldn't release. He gave his name and added, "I wouldn't bother him if this wasn't important."

"We'll see." She waved Jackson inside, told him to wait in the foyer, then glided off to find her husband.

Cranston joined him a few minutes later. "Good thing I already finished dinner. Still, it's Saturday evening and I don't feel like working."

Neither did he. Jackson kept that to himself. "I need to search a homicide suspect's home. I think he either shot his brother or knows who did. After hearing my questions this morning, he may be getting rid of evidence." Jackson handed over the search warrant.

Cranston stared at the papers for a moment, then grudgingly reached for them. "I'll get back to you tomorrow."

Jackson had braced for that. "I believe time is critical, and I'd like to keep moving on this investigation."

The judge glanced through his short summary. "A text? That's all you've got?"

"Sam Turnbull lied and said he hadn't seen or heard from

his brother."

"Maybe he didn't see the text. That's not enough and you know it. Without any physical evidence, you need a lot more circumstantial." Cranston handed back the warrant. "I'll let you subpoena the suspect's phone records, if you want to rewrite this."

He'd expected that response too, but Jackson was still disappointed. He reached in his satchel for the second file he'd prepared. "You know it will take the service provider days to get back to me."

"And *you know* if your victim bled in that house, you'll find proof of it. First you have to convince me he was there."

Jackson's jaw clenched. That was a tough hurdle. Finally he nodded. "Thank you, sir. Have a good evening." He hurried out before he changed his mind and tried to press his case.

On the drive back, he almost went left at the bottom of the hill. He itched to drive out and pick up Sam for questioning. But he knew the man wouldn't go peacefully and wouldn't give up anything during an interrogation. Sam's eyes held a hardness molded by resilience. He'd survived some things—beyond whatever had left those purple scars on the brothers.

Jackson forced himself to go home. Carl was long dead, and his brother was not likely a risk to anyone else. If something happened between them, it had likely been a crime of emotion—anger, fear, or betrayal. Sam Turnbull didn't seem to spend time with other humans who could provoke a violent response. The man might eventually be incarcerated for his part in the crime, but not tonight. Jackson had to be patient and build his case. He might even get some sleep for a change.

Kera was reading in bed when he got home, her long copper hair in a loose braid. "Hey, sweetie. It's nice to see you."

"I'm happy to finally be here. It's been a long day . . . and a tough week." He slid his weapon into the safe and thought about going in to kiss the boys goodnight. *No.* They were sleeping, and he wanted them to stay that way. He thought about their third bedroom. "Is Katie home?"

"Not yet. She's out with Ethan."

"She told me she planned to break up with him." Jackson changed his clothes and climbed into bed. Lying still felt so damn good.

"Maybe she's breaking it to him easy." Kera snuggled next to him. "Want to talk about your day?"

"Nope. Tell me about yours."

She made a dismissive sound. "Nothing worth reporting."

They held each other in silence, Jackson savoring the warmth of her body and the sweet smell of her hair. A sense of peace flooded him, and he closed his eyes. A moment later, Kera slid her hand between his legs. "I've missed you."

How long had it been since they had sex?

Jackson kissed her passionately . . . and remembered a fourth emotion the brothers could have fought about—jealousy. What if a woman had come between them? Their reclusive natures didn't support that idea, so Jackson pushed it out of his mind and reached for Kera's breasts.

His body didn't respond. *Damn.*

"You're distracted. I can tell." She shifted away.

"I'm sorry. I'm just really tired."

"It's okay. Get some sleep and get back to me when you wrap up this case." She kissed him gently and rolled onto her other side.

Jackson lay there, wide awake and frustrated. What was

Sam doing right now?

Let it go!

He closed his eyes and visualized a peaceful scenario. A sunny meadow along a beautiful creek, the ripples creating a soothing melody. Sam popped into the scene, tossing the murder weapon into the water.

Jackson forced the image from his mind and tried again. Steps this time, leading down further and further into the darkness. At the bottom, he spotted a grave.

Crap! This wasn't working.

He climbed out of bed. The only way to know what Sam Turnbull was up to was to keep an eye on him.

Chapter 37

Saturday, 9:35 p.m.

Dallas barely glanced at her new hotel room in Eugene. They were all mostly the same, except for size. She didn't want to think about the space too much. They were all a little depressing. At least on her deep-cover assignments, she lived in apartments or moved in with criminals. The thought brought a sardonic smile to her face. As she brewed coffee in preparation for what could be a long night, her phone rang. *Cameron.* Job protocol told her to ignore it, but her heart ached to hear his sweet, sexy voice.

She snatched up the phone. "Hey, Cam."

"Dallas. You answered. You've been ignoring my texts."

"I was on a plane. Now I'm in Eugene."

"What's going on?"

"I'm about to catch a really bad guy."

He groaned. "Now I'm too worried to sleep. You're not in this alone, right?"

"Of course not." She told him what he needed to hear, but at the moment she felt that way. A Eugene agent hadn't contacted her yet. Dallas tried not to worry. The small field office only employed about eight people, and none were in the office at this hour. Somebody had to be monitoring the phone though. The bureau had never let her down before. "So how was your day?" She tried to keep it casual.

"I got an offer from another brewer to buy me out."

"You're a hot property. Are you going to take it?"

"That's up to you. If I leave Flagstaff and move to Phoenix, I want a commitment that we'll live together."

There it was again. And part of her really wanted to give in this time.

"You're not saying anything."

"The truth is, I'd like it too. But if we live together, I want a commitment that you'll respect my work and not pressure me to quit."

Now he was silent.

"We can talk about this later. I have to get back to work. Love you." She ended the call, her pulse strangely fluttering. She'd just offered to let Cam move in. Was she terrified or excited? Maybe both.

The cure for those feelings waited in a dark, ugly website populated by angry men, and she had to dive back in. First she called the Phoenix bureau and asked to speak to Agent Markley, the cyber tech she'd been working with. He didn't respond, so she left a message: "Dallas again. I'm in Eugene and still need *JungleBoy's* location. I'm also still waiting to hear from a local agent. Can you facilitate that?"

She sat on the bed with her coffee and laptop and checked the No Consent forum. No response from *JungleBoy*. She couldn't believe he'd landed on a dark website without interacting online anywhere else. It was almost logistically impossible. Unless he'd deleted his other social media profiles. Or maybe someone he knew had directed him there.

Just to be thorough, she googled the phrase *social media sites*, scanning for lists. She'd already checked out a dozen, but there were so many more. WeChat, Tumbler, Reddit,

Tagged, Buzznet. The possibilities were endless. Including all the industry- and hobby-specific sites, the task seemed overwhelming. But it would keep her busy until the tech people tracked *JungleBoy's* physical location. If they could. She worried that he might use a proxy server and they might never find him.

Restless, she jogged to a nearby store and bought a bag of salt-and-pepper chips and a six-pack of craft beer she'd never tried before. Back in her room, she opened a bottle, decided it was okay, and got back to work. She checked the No Consent page again to see if her target had responded to her purchase offer.

He had. *JungleBoy*: *U serius? How much will u pay?*

Her pulse jumped. *Hot damn!* He'd taken a huge bite of her bait. Dallas took a moment to think it through and play it right. She was about to offer a predator cash in exchange for a sex slave prisoner. To make the exchange, he would have to show himself—and the woman. Her offer had to be big enough to entice him to take the risk, but not so generous it made him suspicious. What was the asking price for a sex slave? That probably depended on a lot of factors, including the financial level of both parties. Revolting as it seemed, the female's age was likely the biggest consideration for predators in every social bracket.

She messaged back: *What age?*

Dallas took another slug of beer, then stuck the bottle into the mini-fridge. *JungleBoy* probably would want to make the exchange soon, while the rest of the world slept. She needed to be sharp, ready, and flexible.

When she sat back down, he'd already responded: *25? Very pretty, nice tits.*

Ten years too old for most pedophiles and perverts.

Forcing her brain into that mindset, Dallas knocked off a grand from the original number that had popped into her thoughts. In the millionaire world of Jeffrey Epstein and his high-powered friends, a single sexual encounter with a young girl might cost twenty thousand. But *JungleBoy* was a loner incel who might not even have a job. He also seemed open to negotiation. She vacillated for another moment, then settled on a price. Her message read: *3 thou tops but only if she is hot as u say.*

She'd been assigned several criminal scenarios to participate in temporarily, but this one disgusted her more than anything she'd ever done—including plotting an assassination. What a bizarre job!

The perp messaged back: *5 thou and rite now or forget it.*

He wasn't bluffing, she could tell. He wanted the captive out of his life, and he needed a chunk of cash. *JungleBoy* had originally mentioned "trading her in," but maybe he planned to relocate before kidnapping another woman. That would be a good move on his part, but it would make catching him more challenging—especially if he changed his online profile. *Oh hell.* She couldn't mess this up.

As *bi*chgirlhater*, she keyed in her response: *Deal. When and where?*

Dallas stared at the screen, nerves pinging. Any second now she would know exactly where to find him and the woman he'd abducted. Another predator would soon be off the streets. This is what she lived for.

When he didn't respond right away, Dallas munched a few chips and paced the room. *Nothing to worry about.* He was just being careful about choosing a location for the exchange. He might be afraid of being cheated or assaulted.

She sat down and checked her inbox. Still no answer.

Should she message him again? *No.* She might have already made him skittish by seeming too eager. He could be smothering the woman right now, his vehicle packed and ready to roll. *Fuck!*

Dallas paced the room, the coffee kicking in and making her restless.

Where the hell was her backup?

Chapter 38

Saturday, 10:55 p.m.

Jackson drove along Willow Creek, the only thing moving in the dark rural area. A half moon hung in the sky, casting glints of light on the watery marsh landscape. An occasional metal roof tucked against the hillside picked up glimmers too. The quiet aloneness made him question what he was doing out here instead of lying next to a loving woman. He accepted, intellectually, that this was likely a waste of time. Yet until he had Sam Turnbull's phone records and proof that the suspect was still home and working his job, Jackson knew he wouldn't be able to rest.

As he neared the area where he'd found the driveway that morning, Jackson slowed, staring into the shadows for visual cues. Sensing he was near, he shut off his engine. After a few seconds of coasting, he killed his headlights. The tree marking the dirt road loomed ahead, its outline barely visible. Jackson braked and coasted to a stop just off the road.

Now what? He'd texted Evans before leaving his house, asking her to relieve him at dawn. His next task would be to convince Lammers to approve a budget for a full-time surveillance crew. They could use retired detectives who worked the volunteer cold-case squad. Jackson grabbed binoculars from under his seat, eased quietly out of his car, and stepped toward the tree. He might be visible from the house, but not easily. He had approached quietly on the road, so Sam had no reason to look for him.

Even without the field glasses, Jackson could see the truck sitting in the same place under the carport. A soft glow of light peeked out from the edges of the narrow front window. The suspect was likely home. Jackson pulled the binoculars to his eyes and scanned the property. Nothing was amiss that he could tell, but he felt compelled to get closer and look around. Unfortunately, the long driveway offered no cover. In his mind, he saw Sam pick up a shotgun and aim it at him, feeling justified in shooting an intruder. Jackson decided he'd better stay back.

Something glinted in the moonlight at the edge of the carport. Jackson focused his vision until the shape came into view. An aluminum fishing boat. He scanned the wider property, locating a tree about a hundred feet from the house. If he could make it to that shelter undetected, he could . . .

What? Stare at the dark house from a closer vantage point? For what purpose? He remembered how Aaron Russo had gone out the back of his mother's house, so that was a concern. But Sam wouldn't likely leave without his truck. Jackson's phone buzzed in his pocket, startling him. A text. He hurried back to his car and slipped inside.

Evans had messaged him: *Just got back from a run. I'll sleep for three hours, then head your way.*

Her dedication to fitness shamed him. She claimed she jogged late at night to burn off the stress of the job, but he knew it was more than that. She worked her ass off to be strong in every way. Commanding respect in a male-dominated job required it. Jackson texted back: *Thanks. Suspect home, nothing to report. This could be pointless.*

Evans didn't respond, so he figured she was in the shower. An image of her naked, lathered in soap, surfaced in his mind. His body's response was immediate. Jackson shut down the visual and shifted in his seat. *Not helpful!*

Binoculars in hand, he watched the house for a minute from his car. His phone buzzed again, and he glanced down at the screen. Katie this time: *Ethan is acting like a dick and won't get out of my car. Can you help? But no one else! At Rose garden.*

Crap! The guy was a possessive/controlling type, and Katie was at risk of being hurt. Jackson tossed the binoculars on the seat and started his car. He hated leaving the stakeout, but didn't have a choice. Protecting his daughter was primitive—an instinct he had no ability to override.

Jackson told himself that leaving would be all right. The stakeout had just been an impulsive hunch. Sam hadn't left town and didn't seem to be going anywhere or doing anything. As Jackson drove away, he called his daughter.

Katie didn't answer.

Chapter 39

Her ankles shackled again, Bettina lay on the mattress, terrified. She could hear the man upstairs, pacing, muttering, and slamming what sounded like drawers. He'd been doing it off and on for hours with periods of nerve-racking quiet in between. He now considered her "a problem" that needed to be "taken care of." What was he waiting for?

The apprehension made her chest ache. If she was going to die, she would just as soon get it over with. All along, she'd known he might kill her. The commotion she'd heard the day after waking up in this hellhole had been an early warning.

She wouldn't make it easy for him. The baby growing inside her was precious, and she wanted it to have a chance. Weary and shaking, Bettina struggled to her feet and looked around. The depressing room hadn't changed, and no weapon had magically appeared. The only thing new was the bucket. He'd dumped out the warm water to punish her for trying to escape, then thrown the pail down in anger. Now the plastic container lay on its side near the stairs. Bettina shuffled over and picked it up. Hitting him with it would be pointless. What if she slammed it down over his head? Temporarily blinded, the man might flail around just long enough for her to run.

Not with these damn shackles! Fighting back tears, she

tried to think it through. Would he kill her here and drag her body out? Maybe in pieces? Stomach acid burned in her throat at the thought of him hacking at her dead body with an axe. She forced the image out of her mind.

More likely, he would take her somewhere else to do the job. That was more of a risk upfront, during the transport, but safer in the long run because her blood wouldn't be found in his house. What if he forced poison down her throat? She remembered the abduction and chemical smell of the chloroform. He would likely use it again to knock her unconscious, then carry her out. She probably wouldn't ever wake up or know how he'd ended her life.

Unless he buried her alive. *Please God no.*

An idea came to mind. It seemed *loco* and had little chance of working, but she had to try.

His footsteps thumped near the top of the stairs. He was coming! This might be her last few minutes on earth. Heart pounding, Bettina put down the bucket, not wanting to alarm him.

The trapdoor opened, and he came down the steps dressed in dark clothing, a sweatshirt hoodie covering part of his face. The sight made her heart pulse in her throat.

The man paused and stared at her in the dim light. "Why are you standing there?"

Was he worried she would attack him? Bettina choked back a bitter laugh and tried to form words, but her throat was dry and her body trembled with fear.

"Show me your hands!"

Bettina held them out, shaking so hard her teeth chattered. "I'm just scared. Please don't kill me." Her voice gained strength, and now the words tumbled out. "I don't know where I am or who you are. So it's safe to let me go. I have nothing to tell. Please!"

"Shut up!" He stepped toward her. "I wish it didn't have to be like this."

His hand jerked up and she saw the rag. Bettina readied herself, drawing in air. As he pressed the nasty cloth over her nose and mouth, she held her breath. After a moment, she closed her eyes and let her body go slack.

Chapter 40

Sam half dragged, half carried the woman's body up the steps, stopping halfway to catch his breath. This would be the hardest part. After he got her into the truck, the rest would be easier. Well, most of it would. Once he was out there in his safe place, he could take his time. What he had to do next disturbed him, so he'd already shut down the part of his brain that could still feel anything. He'd learned the trick early when his little body was cold, hungry, and in pain—and his mother, the only person who could help him, stood in the corner *purging*, also known as screaming to let out the demons.

At the top of the stairs, he stumbled going through the door, then recovered and threw her body over his shoulder. The woman's weight surprised him. She seemed like such a tiny thing. But she had a chain between her legs and a baby inside her. The thought of the baby dying bothered him more than the woman. For a second, he wondered if he could somehow save it and keep the child for himself.

Stupid!

The baby was one of the reasons he'd changed his mind about selling her to *bi*chgirlhater*. Plus the guy was new to the forum, so Sam didn't trust him yet. What if he lived in Texas? Or Russia? The trade could be slow and risky. Sam wanted this to be over right now. That detective had come snooping around this morning, and he'd seen him check out the pickup. Thank god, he'd fixed the tailgate yesterday. He should have done that before.

Stupid!

Sam crossed through the house and stepped outside. The cold night air made him tense, even though he'd been outside moments ago, loading the truck with a shovel, his guns, and the boat. He'd packed his clothes not long after the cop left.

Now that he was outside, he could smell the rag in his pocket, ready to go again in case Bettina came to and started to struggle. No blood this time. No screw-ups. He was still mad at himself for losing Carl's body out of the back of the truck.

Stupid!

He had wanted to take his beloved little brother far away, where Carl couldn't haunt him. An emotional decision that had cost him. The body had been discovered right away. Sam had thought for a while the police wouldn't connect him to Carl or find him—he was so off the grid. But they had, so now he was screwed.

Sam opened the truck's passenger door and shoved the woman inside. Too bad this hadn't worked out. Now that he'd finally had sex, he wanted more. Lots more. Another guy he knew on the site had kept a woman for years. Sam just couldn't get hard for a pregnant woman. He couldn't let her go either. Bettina had pretended to like him, manipulated him, and betrayed him. *The bitch!*

His online friends were right. Women couldn't be trusted. He'd let himself think for a while that maybe it was just his mother who was untrustworthy and that other fems were different. He'd thought that if he could just meet a girl and spend time with her, she'd see some good in him. But no. They were all cunts. Especially his batshit-crazy mother.

A painful memory pounded his head, dragging him back into the jungle . . . with the heat and sweat and mosquitos.

He'd been four, or maybe five, and didn't really know what life was like for other kids. He knew he missed his father and his toys. All he had was this old suitcase. Sam pushed it around the dirty floor, making an engine sound with his mouth. At least his pretend car could hold a lot of stuff. Well, rocks and knives. That's all he had to play with. His stomach growled, and he looked over at his mother. She stared at her phone, as always, posting. Whatever that meant.

"I'm hungry."

"You can wait until lunch."

He had no idea when that was. "I want a turkey sandwich."

She threw her phone onto the couch and screamed, "I told you to stop asking! We don't eat bread or meat! They're poison!"

Poison was bad, he knew that. But his dad had fed him turkey sandwiches and nothing bad had happened. Sam kept the thought to himself. His mother hated when he brought up the past.

The itching on his arms and legs suddenly became unbearable. Sam scratched a cluster of bug bites on his ankle, digging with his dirty ragged fingernails, hoping to ease the pain.

"Stop scratching!" His mother was suddenly on him, dragging him to the bathtub in the corner. "It's time for a treatment."

She lifted him into the waterless metal tub and pointed a finger. "No screaming or you'll wake the baby."

Sam cringed, wanting to hit her with his fists and run. That would only make things worse. His mother grabbed the scrubbing stone and started to work on the bites he'd just been scratching. Rubbing back and forth, back and forth, the pain unbearable. Sam sobbed and begged her to stop.

"I have to do this. It's the only way to cure staph."

He didn't believe her, because she didn't believe in doctors. But Sam did. One had saved him in the hospital back when his dad was around. But no one could help him now. He had to save himself. *Don't think. Don't feel. It will be over soon.*

Sam pulled himself out of the memory. No wonder he was so messed up. His mother had been heartless, with no ability to offer him empathy or comfort. The bitch had also ruined his fucking teeth, making him hard for women to look at. She'd kept them out of school too, so he was ugly *and stupid.*

Righteous anger propelled him around the front of the truck and into the driver's seat. The woman lay there, head hanging off the bench, her hair still matted into a ponytail. She'd disgusted him with her pleading and lying and smelling so unwashed. Sam started the truck, taking a moment to enjoy the rumble of the engine. A soothing sound that meant escape.

Time to roll.

He glanced at his cargo again. Should he tie her hands together? Maybe before he loaded her into the boat. Right now, she was out cold, and he was anxious to get her away from his house.

He tried not to think about the next hour. Instead, he focused on his future. Where to next? Back to Costa Rica? He both loved and hated the country. When their mother had died and her sister had brought him and Carl back to the states, he'd vowed to never set foot in the muggy mosquito-infested shithole again. But he might not have a choice.

Sam lit a cigarette and drove out the driveway with his lights off, an old habit. When he reached the road, he decided to leave them off. The pond wasn't far away, and he didn't want to attract any attention. That seemed pretty damn unlikely in the middle of the night, but he was done making stupid mistakes.

As he pulled onto the asphalt, the woman suddenly sat up and pushed open the passenger door. Before he could react, she jumped from the truck, stumbled, then started to run.

Chapter 41

The pain in her feet nearly crippling, Bettina sprinted down the dark road, not caring where it led. Her legs felt weak and her brain foggy. Could she keep this up long enough? Earlier in the basement, despite holding her breath, some of the chloroform had entered her system. She could feel it weighing her down. Moments ago, she'd fought to keep from nodding off in the truck as it rolled down the driveway. Now she was more awake, but confused and terrified. Where the hell was she?

A loud engine growled behind her, racing to catch up. Ahead and to the left, she spotted the yellow glow of a light at the base of a hillside. A house! If she could reach it, she might survive. Bettina pushed herself to run faster, but her eyes watered so badly she couldn't see. She veered off the road, looking for a break in the foliage, somewhere to hide.

The truck roared behind her, so close she could feel the engine heat and smell the combustion. Whap! The vehicle struck her from behind. Bettina flew forward, her feet coming off the ground. She landed hard on her chest and skidded, her face scraping the rocky dirt. Bettina struggled to get back up, but she couldn't catch her breath. A truck door slammed nearby, and the man's heavy footsteps bore down.

Chapter 42

Jackson raced back into Eugene, pushing his speed to the limit, glad for the late hour and lack of traffic. At the first main intersection, he rolled through a red light, seeing no reason to stop. As he neared the center of town, a few cars appeared. He slowed, forcing himself to breathe deeply. Fighting to stay calm, he zigzagged across the Whitaker area to avoid stopping.

Katie's location, the Rose Garden, had been planted near a freeway overpass as part of a miles-long park system that stretched along the river. The access street was tucked next to the on-ramp, so the area tended to be quiet, except during spring blooming season or the occasional wedding in the gazebo.

What the hell was Katie doing there in the middle of the night?

Stupid question. She was an eighteen-year-old with a car and a boyfriend and nowhere private to hang out. Jackson prayed she wasn't drunk or stoned. She'd texted him for help, so she had to be thinking somewhat clearly.

Please let her still be there.

As he neared the entrance, his blood roiled. Ethan had better not have hurt his daughter. All of Jackson's training in de-escalation would be thrown out the window. He was a parent first and a cop second. For any father, this could be a worst-case scenario.

He raced down the short dead-end street. A hunched-over figure in a hoodie scurried across, forcing him to brake hard. He squinted into the darkness as the guy ran down a side alley. Not Katie or her boyfriend, more likely an addict out looking to score.

Only one car sat in the parking lot. Katie's Honda. Jackson cut his engine and lights again. This was another situation that might require stealth. He immediately had second thoughts. Maybe flashing lights and a siren would scare the shit out of Ethan. But Jackson didn't want Katie to pay the price. She'd said "no one else." That meant no police, no over-reaction. He still didn't know what to expect, so he eased to a stop behind her car, blocking it in. He could see Ethan in the driver's seat, but where was Katie?

Jackson climbed out and jogged up to the left side of the car. The boyfriend twisted his head, suddenly aware of Jackson's presence, then jerked back and shouted something at the passenger seat. Katie's head popped up, as though she'd been slumped down. *Cowering?* She glanced over at Jackson as he stood next to the window.

For a moment, Ethan refused to acknowledge him. Jackson slammed the butt of his hand against the glass, breaking the silence. The boy finally rolled down the window a few inches. "Mr. Jackson. What's going on?"

He stared past him at Katie, who said casually, "Yeah, Dad, why are you here?"

She wanted to pretend she hadn't summoned him. Was her fear physical or social? Maybe both. It didn't matter. He would play along and do what he had to do. "I told you, Katie. I had a GPS tracking chip inserted into the back of your neck when you were a baby, so I always know where you are." A family joke his daughter was familiar with.

Ethan's mouth dropped open in stunned silence.

Did the dumbass really believe that?

More important, Jackson wanted to know why Katie thought she couldn't just break up with Ethan and drop him off somewhere. Something sketchy was going on—besides this guy's refusal to get out of the car—and his daughter was afraid. "Step out of the vehicle, Ethan, and leave the key."

The young man tried to outstare him, eyes twitching. "That's Katie's decision."

He really *was* stupid. Jackson grabbed the door handle, expecting it to be locked, and it was. He pressed his face against the glass and growled, "I said get out!"

Something flashed in Ethan's lap. Jackson glanced down and saw a cell phone. *Oh shit!* An image of Katie, showing her breasts, beamed up at him from the tiny screen.

Goddamnit! That image was the bastard's leverage.

Jackson shoved his hand through the small opening above the glass and grabbed Ethan by the hair. "Unlock the door and get out of the car." He spoke slowly, a cold rage seething.

"Okay! Okay! You don't have to get all jacked up." The kid finally complied, awkwardly climbing out. When Ethan was on his feet, Jackson let go, but left the door open. Ethan rubbed his head and scowled. "Nothing's going on."

"Put your hands in the air! Leave the phone on the seat!" Jackson shouted like he was dealing with a hardened criminal.

Ethan glanced over at Katie, but she wouldn't look at the boy. Jackson hoped she was smart enough to grab the phone as soon as the jackass put it down.

"Hey, this is just a misunderstanding," Ethan whined, still gripping his cell.

"Empty your hands and put them up!"

He dropped the phone and kicked it under the car.

Good enough. Jackson stepped forward—and smelled alcohol on Ethan's breath. "Turn around."

"Come on, man. This isn't cool."

No shit. Jackson grabbed his shoulder and spun him around. As he cuffed Ethan's wrists, he heard Katie's door open.

"I'm arresting you for *minor in possession.*" The brat's parents would likely post bail and have him home before daylight, but Jackson didn't care. As long as Katie deleted those stupid images and broke free of the relationship.

"This is bullshit!" Even shouting, Ethan sounded whiny.

Jackson guided him, none too gently, toward the back of his police sedan. He glanced over his shoulder at Katie, who was running around the front of her car. *Good.* She was getting the phone. As Ethan climbed into the backseat, he shouted into the darkness. "This isn't over, Katie! I love you!" His frustration was obvious.

Jackson had a flash of sympathy. As he slid behind the wheel, he saw his daughter crawl on the ground, her arm under the car, searching for the phone and its blackmail content. His empathy disappeared and another flash of rage hit him.

Katie got her hands on the device and stood, holding it up for him to see. She mouthed "Thank you" and rubbed her hand over her heart.

Jackson changed his mind, got out, and hurried over. "Katie, I'm sorry you had to learn this the hard way, but relationships are almost never permanent. Fifty percent of all marriages end in divorce. A person who loves you today might hate you next month. Never give anyone that much power." He squeezed her in a tight hug, then ran back to his car.

Relieved, he started his engine and backed out. Irritation quickly set in. He didn't have time for this crap and still had to drop off Ethan at the jail.

After that, he would race back out to Willow Creek and sit in the dark, watching another sketchy guy—who hopefully hadn't done anything criminal in the meantime. Jackson sighed. Were there any good guys left in the world?

Chapter 43

Dallas shoved her laptop aside. *JungleBoy* had gone silent. She vacillated between blaming herself for not handling the communication well and accepting that he was an unpredictable sociopath who might not have been serious about her offer from the beginning. People said all kinds of things online that had no truth or basis in reality. They did it for sport, shock value, or to make themselves feel better in the moment.

She'd spent the last hour perusing the Not Normal and No Consent sites, searching for any info that could lead her to *JungleBoy*—and came up with nothing. She had found a few more men who needed to be tracked down and arrested. A sub-thread of messages by *KingCockXXX* were particularly disturbing.

For the moment, she couldn't read another misogynistic post. They were making her hate men—and doubt women too. Were any of the claims the incels made true? If so, she wanted to slap the women who'd treated them that way. Dallas paced her small hotel room, too hyped to sleep. Somewhere in this area, an angry, socially inept man had kidnapped a woman for his own sexual pleasure and now he wanted to "trade her in." If she didn't find *JungleBoy* soon, another woman would experience that trauma. Based on what she'd read by others on the site and occasional news reports about abductees who managed to escape, hundreds of women might face that risk. The thought horrified her.

She called her cyber tech again. He picked up and grumbled, "I'm working on it, but the perp uses a VPN, so it's taking time."

"Sorry." She realized the cyber guy hadn't slept much either. "I'm going out for a quick run, but I'll have my phone."

"I'll text you when I have him."

"Thanks."

Dallas tried the Eugene field office again, but nobody answered. She thought about waking her boss in Phoenix but changed her mind. At the moment, she didn't actually need any support. The sex-slave deal with *JungleBoy* had fallen through, and she still had no idea where he was. Still, it was unsettling that her breaking case seemed to have fallen through the bureaucratic cracks. Dallas wasn't worried for herself. *JungleBoy* was a loner, not part of an organized criminal ring—but a woman's life was at stake.

There was always the Eugene police. They had patrol officers on the streets, even in the middle of the night, but she couldn't call them for help until she had an active criminal situation. By then, it might be too late.

Unable to stay in the room a moment longer, Dallas changed into athletic shoes. According to the hotel's website, a bike-and-walking path ran along a canal right behind the property. She hurried downstairs and jogged through the lobby toward the back door. The desk clerk, a twenty-something man, snuck glances at her as she passed. With only a few hours sleep in the previous days, Dallas didn't feel attractive, but her body hadn't changed and her running clothes fit snugly.

She crossed the tiny patch of grass to the concrete path and ran west. The lights along the nearby main street gave her enough illumination to see that the left bank sloped down to a little creek. Moonlight shimmered on the slow-moving water. Feeling uncertain about taking a break from work—and missing a response from *JungleBoy*—she stopped and set her phone timer for fifteen minutes. She would turn around when the alarm went off, giving her a two-and-a-half-mile run.

Moving forward again, she thought about tracking her miles on a more regular basis, just for fun. She didn't want or need a FitBit, but there were some apps she could download to her phone that would be even better. One called Strava allowed users to map and record their routes. She didn't want her data to be stored online for others to see, so that wouldn't work for her.

Dallas stopped short. Strava was a social media site. With maps! She hadn't searched it yet for *JungleBoy*. What was the chance he was a fitness fanatic? Slim to none. She scoffed and started to run again. She would check it when she got back.

A moment later, she stopped again.

The site stored users' running and biking routes. What if predators used that data to track female athletes and figure out where to encounter someone they were stalking? A chill ran through her body. Even if *JungleBoy* didn't access Strava, other incels might. She needed to include the site in her investigation. Dallas raced back to the hotel.

After downing a glass of water, she logged into the app and quickly filled out a profile as Amber Davison. She uploaded an undercover photo and gave the Vancouver address the bureau had established. Once she was a member, she keyed her target's screen name into the search field.

Seconds later, there he was. *JungleBoy's* online profile.

Adrenaline rushed through her veins. She clicked the Follow button, then scrolled through his scanty information. The address listed turned out to be the local newspaper, so that was no help. She accessed a link to his exercise maps. The perp had only posted twice, about four months earlier, and the routes both began and ended on Willow Creek Road. Most likely his house.

Her pulse thumped in her throat. Unless he'd moved recently, she'd finally located him.

Chapter 44

Sam pressed the cloth over Bettina's face for a full ten seconds this time, hoping it still had enough chemical to work. She dropped like a stone. The bitch might never wake up again. Would he even have to shoot her? Maybe he could just bury her like this. Or strangle her in the truck to prevent this shit from happening again. The thought gave him an uneasy feeling. He didn't want to be this person. He just wanted sex like everyone else.

He dragged her out of the ditch, glancing around nervously. They were alone out here in the middle of the night.

With her body over his shoulder, he carried her to the pickup, stumbling under the weight. His heart pounded so hard it worried him. Maybe he should cut back on his smoking. He wanted to take the easy route and toss her in the back, but he'd learned his lesson on that one. With the passenger door open, he heaved her onto the seat and shoved her legs in after. Loading Carl, who was a lot heavier, into the back of the truck had required a stepstool and had still been a nightmare. Never again, he promised himself.

Could he hold to that? In Costa Rica, grabbing girls would be even easier. If he chose the right ones, nobody would even look for them. If he got bored or annoyed with one, others would be there for the taking. But he shouldn't think about that now.

Focus!

He slammed the door closed and ran around to the other side. He just needed to drive a fast mile down the road, park behind the blackberry tangle, and get her into the boat. Once he was on the water, he would be safe.

At the pull-off site, Sam unloaded the skiff first. As he reached for the tie line, a wave of memories paralyzed him. Carl as a child, laughing as they played in the creek by their primitive jungle home. The two of them, right here in this spot, getting ready to go out fishing, and Carl teasing him about his fear of water. His brother had laughed then too, a joyful sound that always softened the middle of Sam's chest. How would he live without him? He should have let the woman go and forced Carl to leave town with him. His little brother would have gone along. No, that wouldn't have worked out. The way Carl had looked at him after discovering his secret—Sam had known things between them would never be the same.

An unexpected sob escaped his body. *Goddamnit, Carl!* Why couldn't he have just minded his own business? But his brother had snooped in the basement. What choice had that left him? The memory of that horrible moment was never far from his mind. For a second, Sam was breathless, paralyzed while it washed over him.

The day had been warm, the last of the summer heat, and he'd gone to the store for groceries. When Sam arrived home, Carl's car was parked next to his truck. *Shit!* What was he doing here? Sam rushed inside, wishing he'd changed the locks after he kicked his brother out.

Carl stood in the living room, hands on his hips, like always when he was upset about something, his face ashen. "Who is that in the basement, Sam?"

Oh fuck. He knew. "You don't live here anymore!" Sam tried to intimidate his younger brother as only he could. "You can't just come in and dig around in my stuff."

"I wanted to see you. I've missed hanging out." For a moment, Carl looked sad, but then he shook it off. "Don't change the subject. This is serious shit! You can't keep a woman in your basement!"

"Shut up! This isn't your business." Sam instinctively moved toward the kitchen, positioning himself between his brother and the pantry. Still, he hoped to appease Carl, who liked to grab onto things like a dog with a rope, sometimes biting down until he hurt himself. Sam softened his voice as best he could. "I'm gonna let her go, I promise. It's just a game."

Carl narrowed his eyes. "Who is she? What game?"

"Forget it. It's just a sex thing. I met a woman online like you said I should." Sam beamed, like he was proud of himself. Carl was so naive, so uneducated, he would probably believe him.

"Why is she locked in?"

"It's part of the game. Some women like that kind of thing."

His brother's eyes flickered, thinking hard. But he didn't get on board. "I don't believe you. Sorry, Sam, but this is messed up. You have to let her go."

"You're the one who's messed up. Don't judge me."

"It's not the same. Not even close. And I'm clean again." Carl's lips trembled. "Don't make me fight you. Don't make me tell."

Sam stiffened, feeling himself shift into survival mode. *Don't think, don't feel, just get through this.* "You're overreacting. She's not important."

"She's a person! If you won't let her go, I will."

"No! I'm not going to prison." Sam reached for the shotgun in the rack by the pantry. "Get out!"

"You gonna shoot me?" Carl's face contorted into shock, then pain and disbelief. Lips still trembling, his brother stared, as though he could will Sam to change his mind.

Suddenly, his brother charged, that bulldog look on his face.

Without thinking, Sam lifted the shotgun and fired.

The look of shock on Carl's face would never fade from his mind. Sam shook off the memory. Killing his brother—his family, the only person he loved—had wrecked him. Ripped out what was left of his heart and shit on it. Sam hadn't slept or eaten well since.

If only he could go back in time, he would have never joined that online group. That was the old man's fault. He'd told him about the forums and opened a door that Sam couldn't resist. He'd been sucked in hard and fast. He'd even kicked Carl out of the house once he'd made the plan. The sex had been worth it. No one should have to live their whole life without ever experiencing that crazy intensity. If only he didn't have these scars and rotten teeth, thanks to his crazy mother who didn't believe in soap or toothpaste . . .

Focus!

Sam forced himself to stop thinking and drag Bettina's body out of the pickup and into the boat. With a tie line in hand, he started pulling the heavy load down the dirt path to the pond. Boy, would his arms be sore tomorrow. He'd originally planned to bury her behind the house, which belonged to his aunt. But that damn cop had showed up. Sam had been worried sick ever since. He knew the guy would be back and maybe bring one of those dogs that could smell blood and dead bodies.

This was his only option.

At the edge of the water, he stopped and checked on the woman. Her breath shallow, she appeared unconscious. Sam lifted her head and dropped it to make sure. When her face thudded on the boat's bottom, she made a soft sound but didn't wake up. *Stupid!* He wouldn't do that again.

Sam tossed the line into the hull, grabbed the side, and gave a shove. He climbed in, reached for an oar, and started to row. He wished he could dump her over the side into the water, but that was a good way to capsize a small aluminum boat. And he'd never learned to swim. Not after nearly drowning in the ocean while his mother sat on the beach looking at her cell phone.

Burying the woman out here was too much work and too risky. So was transporting a dead body, he'd learned. At least the pond was close. After this, he'd hit the road and not look back.

Chapter 45

As he reached the main east/west intersection, Jackson almost veered toward home. The stakeout at Sam's house suddenly felt like an impulsive waste of time. He'd just been frustrated and too wired to sleep. His brain was still functioning, but his body had hit the wall. It was the middle of the damn night, and he was getting too old for this shit.

Yet he'd asked Evans to relieve him at dawn, and he couldn't call her off. She was getting some much-needed sleep at the moment, and he wouldn't interrupt her. He would suck it up and survive a few more hours of surveillance. After that, he planned to rest for a few hours himself, then harass midlevel service managers until they sent the brothers' phone records.

Jackson made the turn and headed west instead.

Twelve minutes later, as he neared Sam's driveway, he spotted a small car sitting off the road. Jackson slowed, squinting into the gloomy landscape. What was that about? This whole area was undeveloped and mostly unpopulated, with only a few homes and no parks or public attractions. In his police officer mindset, anyone driving around after midnight was suspect, either looking to score drugs or steal something. He didn't care about a drug deal beside the road, but instinct told him this was something different.

A moment later, he spotted someone moving diagonally across the field between the parked car and Sam's house. The intruder kept low and moved quickly in the open spaces between shrubs. *What the hell?*

He rolled to a stop in the same place as before and climbed out, binoculars in hand. He tried to spot the intruder, but couldn't. Jackson hustled over to the open space in the dirt driveway and trained his field glasses on Sam's property.

The truck was gone!

Crap! Heart pounding, he sprinted down the driveway, not caring if anyone saw him. He tried to work through possible scenarios, but nothing made sense. As he neared the house, he reached for his weapon. Should he have taken a moment to call for backup? He didn't know. This could be nothing, maybe just a Peeping Tom. Yet if the brothers were drug runners, something serious could be happening. A competitor trying to steal a major stash while Sam wasn't home. Jackson's gut told him the suspect wasn't coming back. He'd blown it by leaving and wanted to kick himself.

Abruptly, the intruder stepped out from behind a tree. Slender, dressed in dark clothes—and pointing a gun at him.

"FBI. Drop your weapon!"

What? Did he know that voice? He wouldn't stand down, not yet. "Eugene Police!"

"Jackson?" She moved toward him, her weapon now aimed at the ground.

He struggled to place her for a moment, then a memory surfaced. She was the undercover agent who'd helped his team take down an eco-terrorist. He couldn't remember her name though. "What are you doing here?"

"Tracking a sexual predator." She glanced around the empty driveway. "And he seems to be gone."

"Sam Turnbull?"

"If that's his name. I only know him online as *JungleBoy*."

Jackson's thoughts raced. "Let's step out of the clearing. Sam might still be in the house, and I'm pretty sure he owns a shotgun."

They scurried sideways until they were obscured in the shadows of an oak tree. "Agent Dallas, by the way." She nodded, but her expression didn't change. Even in the partial moonlight with her hair tucked into a knit cap, she was stunning. Deadly too, if he remembered correctly.

"What do you mean by sexual predator?" Jackson felt stupid asking.

"He kidnapped a woman to keep as a sex slave." A grunt of disgust. "Then offered to sell her. But I think I spooked him." She swore under her breath. "I still hope to find her."

Blood rushed out of Jackson's head, and his mouth went dry. "What woman?" Had Sam, or maybe Carl, taken Bettina? She was the only active missing-person case he knew about. The other woman from the Target parking lot had been located.

"I don't know anything about her." Dallas tucked her weapon into the holster under her sweater. "We got a tip from another predator in Vancouver, but all I've had to work with since are online postings."

"Her name might be Bettina Rios."

"You're looking for her here?" The agent gestured toward the home.

"I am *now*. I also suspect Sam of shooting his brother."

She seemed taken aback for a second. "Let's find the son-of-a-bitch." She twitched, as though she couldn't hold back. "His captive might still be alive."

"And in that house," Jackson added. "I'll call for an ATL on

Sam's truck."

"I'm going in." Dallas took off running.

Jackson pressed 911 and started after her. As he jogged, he relayed his request to a dispatcher, trying to breathe normally. "I need an attempt to locate. Brown 2004 Chevy pickup belonging to Sam Turnbull." He visualized the license plate number and recited it. "Vehicle last seen in the Willow Creek area west of Eugene." Jackson ended the call and picked up his pace.

Dallas, already at the door, spun to face him. "Dead-bolted. Let's try the back."

She raced around the house, fast and sure-footed, despite the darkness. Jackson followed, passing the windows on the side, thinking they could break one if needed.

The back door gave way as they shouldered it together. They charged inside, weapons drawn. "Police!" Jackson called out. "Show yourself!"

The shadowy house remained silent, the smell of disinfectant burning his eyes. Jackson fumbled along the wall and flipped a switch. A light came on, revealing a nearly empty space. Only a couch and a small TV propped on a wooden crate.

"Doesn't look like he lived here long," Dallas said, jogging into the hall.

Jackson strode into the kitchen. A swinging door at the end suggested a pantry. He strode toward it, with the sinking feeling that Sam and his captive were gone. Would he take Bettina out of state or dump her somewhere along the way? Dallas had mentioned that Sam tried to sell the woman online. Maybe her value as a sex slave would keep her alive.

He passed empty kitchen counters that smelled like 409 cleaner and entered the pantry. The light had been left on, but the shelves were nearly bare. Only a few canned goods. He stepped back to leave and felt the floor shift under him. Jackson looked down, noticing a rectangular outline. An opening!

He felt around under the bottom pantry shelf until he found the braided-rope handle. With his fingers wrapped around it, he slid the rope out into the open and pulled. The hinged trapdoor squeaked as it rose, revealing a set of stairs.

Dallas came up behind him. "What did you find?"

"A basement." Jackson stepped onto the first rung.

"Be careful," Dallas called. "I'll stay here and keep watch."

Smart. Getting locked down there would be a nightmare, as poor Bettina had probably experienced. He descended slowly, using his cellphone flashlight to illuminate the underground room. Concrete walls, with only a mattress and half a loveseat. Plus a bucket in the corner. The stench told him what it was for.

A quick perimeter search didn't reveal additional openings or rooms. Crossing back, his light picked up bloodstains on the floor. They looked fresh. Had Sam hurt her? Jackson remembered Bettina had been pregnant. Maybe she had miscarried. So many lives ruined by one man's sexual compulsion. The realization sickened him. Jackson's distress morphed into anger as he hurried up the stairs, determined to find and punish Sam Turnbull. "She *was* here, but not now."

"No clothes or personal items," Dallas reported. "He's on the run."

As Jackson had suspected. "Let's go get the bastard."

They moved through the house carefully, taking another look. It didn't take long. Sam had lived a minimalist life.

Outside, Jackson glanced around, his vision limited by the lack of exterior lights. Yet he sensed something was different.

The carport was empty. It took a moment to realize what that meant. "The boat's gone."

"What?" Dallas spun back, puzzled.

"When I was here earlier, there was an aluminum skiff under the carport."

"He left his TV but took his boat?" Dallas pulled off her cap and rubbed her scalp. "Does that make sense?"

"Only if you need the boat for something specific." Images and case notes came together for him. The moss on Carl Jagger's boots. The pond he'd seen that morning. The skiff now in the back of Sam's truck. "He plans to dump her in the water." Jackson took off running.

Dallas quickly matched his step. "A lake around here somewhere?"

"A pond just down the road. We both passed it on the way in."

"I'll follow you in my car." She paused, barely breathing hard. "In case we need both vehicles to box him in."

"I'll call for backup."

Jackson stopped at his sedan, contacted dispatch, and got the same call-taker. "Jackson again. I need my team and patrol units." The exact address escaped him. "A pond two miles west of Eighteenth on Willow Creek." He started to hang up, then added, "Maybe send a motorboat."

"We don't have one, but I'll call the sheriff's department."

Jackson climbed into his car, while Dallas ran down the road to hers. As he raced along the unlit road, searching the wetlands for a truck or a pond, he tried to visualize how this would play out. He had no idea what to expect—and wondered if he could even find the right pond. He'd spotted several on his daylight trip out here, but only one seemed big enough to dump a body in.

Shimmering glints of light flickered ahead and off to the right. Movement, for sure. Was it an aluminum skiff catching moonlight? He let off the accelerator and pumped the brakes to signal Dallas behind him. Finding the access in the dark would be challenging. He slowed to a crawl, watching for a gravel patch or a break in the foliage.

There! An area that seemed to be both.

He slowed again and eased to the side, driving half off the pavement. Once he cleared a massive patch of blackberries, he eased slowly off the road. His tires crunched the gravel for a moment, then went quiet as the ground gave way to dirt and grass. Where was Sam's truck?

He braked, scrambled out, and scanned the area. As he stared back at the road, he spotted it, tucked in behind the towering blackberry tangle. Jackson's hammering pulse eased, just knowing the suspect was still in range, relieved that he hadn't let a sociopath get away by abandoning his stakeout earlier.

Dallas ran softly toward him. "The pond is out there, through those willows." She pointed, her voice an excited whisper. "I catch glimpses of his movement on the water."

Now what? They needed searchlights, a rescue boat, maybe even a canine unit. Anxiety squeezed his chest, pushing his heart to race again. By the time they had the resources needed to pull this off, they would be too late to save Bettina, and Sam Turnbull could be long gone.

Chapter 46

Dallas quickly assessed the situation. "Call for a search team and a helicopter. I'm going after him." She spotted a break in the grass and kept moving, running down the barely visible dirt path. Embedded rocks threatened to trip her, so she watched the ground as she ran.

Footsteps behind her as Jackson called out, "You mean swim?"

What else? She didn't intend to stand on the shore and watch as a predator dumped a body out there and got away. What if the woman wasn't dead? He might have another vehicle stashed on the other side of the pond. He might be trying to fake both their deaths so he could take her out of state—and sell her to another incel.

The horrific life of a captive was never far from her thoughts when she was undercover. She'd been in several situations where she could have ended up in that position. As long as she had strength and breath, she would chase this guy.

She glanced up from the rocky ground and stared into the distance. She could see him now, out there rowing slowly. *Was that an island?*

At the water's edge, she peeled off her shoes, sweater, and holster, with the palm-sized handgun still in it. Jackson arrived, a little winded, and she handed him the weapon. "There's an island out there, so I think he plans a stop."

She pivoted and stepped into the shallow water. Her feet hit a semi-solid bottom of mud and grass, and the cold sent a shock through her system. This would be ugly. She rushed forward until she was waist deep, then lunged into a swim. The icy water penetrated her thin tank-top, and her whole body tightened. *If you're cold, you're not working hard enough!* An FBI bootcamp trainer had liked to yell that. Dallas pumped and kicked harder, keeping her face just above the water. She didn't want to know what was below her. The sour, murky smell was bad enough.

She tried to form a plan as she plowed across the pond but couldn't focus enough. Her brain was in function-only mode and just kept chanting *stroke, stroke, stroke.* As she neared the island, she worried about how much noise she was making. Would the perp be standing on the shore with a gun, waiting to kill her instantly?

Dallas switched to a quiet breaststroke and kept going. With her head more upright, she noticed the boat sat a hundred yards ahead, half out of the water. She didn't see Sam or the woman.

A few minutes later, Dallas made contact with something solid, brought her feet up under her, and stood. As she trudged past the little skiff, she stared at the oars, still in their clamps. Could she use one as a weapon?

Maybe. They were too long and heavy to swing like a bat, but if she gripped the wooden paddle in the middle she could use it like a joust. With a cold shaky grip, she eased one out of its metal ring, trying not to make a sound. Dallas heaved it onto her shoulder and took the last few steps out of the water.

Finally she was on dry land, cold wet yoga pants clinging to her legs. She glanced around, looking for something shorter and heavier to use as a weapon. The shrubby foliage on the island didn't offer much, except to obscure what little vision she had. She couldn't even tell how big the island was.

A sound cut through the darkness. Clink. Clink. Clink.

A shovel hitting hard dirt.

Shit! He was prepping to bury a body. That meant he'd already killed his captive. Dallas picked up a fist-sized rock in her free hand. A better weapon for close-up combat, which was not her best strength. With a little daylight and a sniper rifle, she could have picked him off from the back of his truck on shore.

Clink. Clink. Clink. The rhythmic sound continued as she squat-walked through the bushes, keeping her weapons ready. The foliage thinned, and she could now see his outline and jerky movements. Beyond him about twenty yards, the water glistened, but she couldn't tell how far it went.

Dallas dropped to her belly and crawled to the edge of the clearing, awkwardly dragging the oar. The open patch of soft earth was about thirty feet across, and Sam stood in the middle. To his left about ten feet, a shadowy form lay on the ground. Dallas worried that if the killer turned, he might see her pale arms. But he didn't look over, just kept digging.

Where was his shotgun?

She scanned the ground, not seeing it, but a smaller shape caught her eye. A handgun? That gave her better odds. At this close range, she would be hard to miss with scatter shot. The small weapon lay halfway between the man and the body. Could she get to it before he did?

His voice cut through the darkness. "Good enough." He stopped digging and seemed to stare straight at her. Dallas tensed, ready to roll sideways and spring to her feet.

Sam abruptly threw down his shovel, snatched up the handgun, and aimed it at the body on the ground.

The woman was still alive?

Chapter 47

For a moment, Jackson hesitated. He needed to be in two places at the same time—close to the road so he could signal their location when patrol officers arrived, but also in the water. He couldn't let Dallas confront a killer, unarmed, without any backup. Somehow he had to do both.

As he sprinted to his car, a plan came together in his head. He popped the trunk and grabbed a flare, hoping he remembered how to use it. The cap! He pulled off the plastic end and rotated it in his palm. Holding the flare steady with his other hand, he struck the two ends together as if lighting a giant match. A flame erupted instantly. He tossed the flare toward the road and pivoted back to his car.

His other idea was less certain, but he had to try. Jackson grabbed a large evidence bag from his satchel, shoved his weapon inside, and closed the ziplock seal. He searched for a second container, but none were large enough.

Now for the hard part. He charged down the narrow path, stumbling over rocks as he ran. At the pond's edge, Jackson scanned the inky water and saw Dallas, swimming like a pro, halfway to the island.

He peeled off his jacket and shoes, dreading what came next. He hadn't been swimming since he was a teenager, and even then the sport hadn't appealed to him much. He'd gone along to keep his friends happy.

Today, it might save a life . . . or end his.

Jackson picked up the plastic bag. How best to carry his weapon? He shoved it down the back of his pants, where it was least likely to fall out, then emptied his pockets and sucked in a deep breath. Lives were at stake. Not only in the moment, but the future as well. They couldn't let Sam escape and terrorize other women. Sexual predators never just stopped on their own.

He could do this!

Jackson charged forward. Plunging into the icy pond gave him second and third thoughts, but he kept going, churning his arms like a crazed man. *Damn, it was cold!*

He shut down his brain, went into autopilot, and pushed himself harder than he ever had. Time seemed to stand still, and he had no idea how long he was in the water. Finally he allowed himself to look up. There was Sam's boat, and beyond it, the island. Relief washed over him and he swam ashore.

Chapter 48

As he aimed the gun at Bettina, a tremor traveled up Sam's arm and into his heart. *What the fuck?* Why was this so hard? He should have killed her already. At this point, she was just a headache he didn't need. But when she'd been nice to him, he'd started to like her—and her poor baby hadn't done anything wrong.

Stupid! Just do it!

Sam started to squeeze the trigger, but footsteps pounded behind him. Shocked, he spun and saw a woman in black coming at him with an oar. Only a few feet away! His heart skipped a beat, but he instinctively lifted the weapon and squeezed again.

A deafening boom filled the air, just as the oar slammed into the side of his head. For a split second, pain blinded him, then morphed into rage. He would beat her to death for that, whoever the hell she was.

Chapter 49

Pain exploded in Dallas' leg. For a moment, she couldn't think or move. A primitive survival instinct kicked in and she pushed past it. He was coming at her with a murderous look, blood dripping from his forehead, gun still in hand.

There was nowhere to run, and the oar was on the ground behind him. She'd lost it on impact.

Dallas lunged with her whole body, bashing the rock into his face at the same time.

"Bitch!" He staggered back, as her momentum knocked them both to the ground.

She landed on top, and his weapon slammed into the dirt. Dallas lifted her arm and plunged the rock down onto his gun hand.

Sam screamed and pushed her off.

They struggled to their feet, blood running. Sam lurched for the gun, but Dallas blocked him, kicking the weapon at the same time. It skidded toward the shackled woman.

Chapter 50

Jackson stepped onto the rocky shore, grateful to be out of the water. His breath ragged, he bent over and sucked in oxygen. He'd never been so cold, so winded, but he had to keep moving. Dallas was here somewhere and needed his help.

He jogged forward, reaching for the gun bag in the back of his pants. He ripped open the plastic and grabbed his Sig Sauer. It felt damp in his hand. *Please let it still be working.* He took another step, and a gunshot rang out.

No! Jackson broke into a sprint, charging through the chest-high shrubs toward the sound. His wet clothes clung in places and slapped his skin in others, but he couldn't let the baggage slow him down. When he broke free of the bushes, he saw Dallas and Sam twenty feet away. The agent lay on her back near a shallow grave, bleeding from her thigh. Sam straddled her, pounding her face with his fist. His nose gushed blood too. Jackson didn't see a gun anywhere.

He charged forward, his weapon pointed at Sam's head. "Police! Stop or I'll shoot!"

The man looked up, startled. In a sudden move, he rolled sideways, then scrambled to his hands and knees, like a wild monkey. In a split second, he disappeared into a tangle of vegetation. A glimmer of daylight on the horizon revealed the edge of the island beyond it.

"Freeze! Or I'll shoot!" Jackson bolted after him. Could he hit the moving target? He could only see Sam's body in intervals, as he ducked in and out of the bushes. A moment later, the man was on his feet, running toward the water.

Goddamnit! Jackson followed, hating to shoot anyone in the back—but he had no choice. With both hands on his cold weapon, Jackson pulled the trigger.

Click.

The gun had misfired. He tried again. Another fail. *Crap!* He would have to run the perp down.

Movement to his right made him jump. Jackson pivoted, still aiming the useless weapon. The captive woman, wrists and ankles shackled, struggled to stand.

Was that a handgun?

She stretched out her arms and fired.

Boom!

Jackson spun back to face the pond. The kidnapper stumbled but didn't go down, staggering toward the pond.

Bettina fired again.

The bullet hit Sam's back, and he pitched face down in the shallow water. For a moment, he struggled to crawl, but soon his body lay still.

Jackson ran to Bettina as she collapsed to her knees, sobbing. She looked unharmed, so he pivoted back to Dallas.

Blood oozed from her thigh, but she was conscious and propped up on her elbows. "We got him." Her voice was weak, but a small laugh escaped her throat.

Jackson ripped off his shirt, knelt down, and tied a tourniquet around her thigh. Overhead, the sound of a helicopter made them both look up. Help was coming.

Chapter 51

Monday, September 23, 11:45 a.m.

Jackson ordered enough pizza to feed an army, plus Schak, and wished he could offer everyone a beer too. The last week had been insane, and his team had worked tirelessly on two cases. But Lammers wouldn't appreciate alcohol in the department at noon, and Schak was trying to stay sober. So Jackson would wait until later to indulge in his occasional libation. Maybe he and Evans could go out for a celebratory drink after work. *No.* He had to stop thinking about her.

Jackson's phone rang. *Sophie again.* He knew what she wanted, and he didn't blame her. He had a few minutes before the meeting, so he answered. "Hey, Sophie. Let's make this quick."

"What the hell went down yesterday morning? Or I should say *up.*" She was so eager, she sounded breathless. "Who was airlifted in the police helicopter?"

"Bettina Rios, the missing woman whose picture has been in the news." He already regretted taking the call but felt committed. "She'd been kidnapped and held captive for a week."

"Holy shit!" Her computer keys clicked madly in the background. "Who took her?"

"Sam Turnbull, the brother of the homicide victim."

"That's wild. I assume the crimes were connected?" A slight pause. "Sam killed Carl to silence him?"

"That's our assumption too. We'll never know for sure because Sam died in the confrontation."

"Police shot him?"

"Bettina did." Jackson glanced at the clock. "It's a long story, and I don't have time right now."

"Please don't do that to me." Stress in her voice now. "Promise you'll tell me later."

"You can ask Bettina when she's feeling better." Jackson knew Sophie planned to do that anyway. "I really have to go."

"Wait! Why did he abduct her? Was it a possessive sex-girl in the basement thing?"

"Exactly." Jackson ended the call, the only way to get Sophie off the line.

"Who were you talking to?"

Jackson swiveled to see Evans standing in the cubicle opening, smiling.

"Sophie. She's been calling obsessively." He smiled back. "Did you get some sleep yesterday?"

"Went to bed at nine last night and slept until six this morning. I've never done that before."

Jackson laughed. "I was asleep at seven, but didn't make it past five a.m. We have a loud, early riser."

"Micah?"

"Yeah." He stood. "Let's head for the conference room." He put his phone on vibrate-only as they walked.

Lammers entered the foyer at the same time. "You both look like hell. Maybe head out early today."

Her way of giving them time off—without having to be nice about it.

"Will do," Schak said, walking up. "I could use a whole

week off too."

Lammers rolled her eyes, and they headed into the meeting hall. The sergeant took the seat at the head of the table where Jackson usually sat. He didn't care. Both cases had wrapped up and he'd had a full night's sleep, so he was feeling good. Mostly.

"Where's lunch?" Schak looked around with mock concern.

"It's not that kind of meeting." Jackson gave him an exaggerated wink.

Lammers cleared her throat. "Give me the update. I have my own work to do."

Jackson glanced at the case notes he'd updated earlier, but he didn't need to. "There are details about these crimes we'll never know. Our best hypothesis is that Sam Turnbull stalked and kidnapped Bettina Rios, then killed his brother Carl when he discovered his secret."

"Sam is dead?" Lammers asked.

"Yes. After we intervened, his captive shot him and he landed in the water." The image would probably never leave his mind. The whole scenario had haunted his dreams the night before.

Schak leaned in. "I still don't understand the connection. If Sam was such a recluse, how did he meet Bettina?"

Jackson was still struggling with that. A clumping sound filled the doorway, and Agent Dallas limped into the room, using a cane. She tried to smile, but her pain was obvious. "Sorry to be late. I'm moving a little slow."

"That happens when you get shot." Evans made an appreciative sound. "You're such a badass."

"The bullet just tore some flesh." Dallas hobbled to a chair. "Still hurts like hell, but no structural damage."

Jackson stared at the agent, admiring her courage and tenacity. He also hoped she had information to share. "Do you know how Sam latched onto Bettina?"

"An exercise app called Strava, where people log their routes and connect for group events." Dallas winced as she sat down. "Sam, aka *JungleBoy,* was following Bettina and knew her jogging routine."

The tree-shrouded park entrance flashed in Jackson's mind. It had been Sam waiting for her there, not her ex-boyfriend. Had Aaron Russo killed himself because they were wrong? *No.* Jackson pushed the guilt aside. The young man had committed suicide out of despair in losing her.

Dallas broke into a grin. "That app is also how I found Sam. He logged a few routes months ago, and they told me exactly where to find him."

"Digital karma." Lammers snorted. "You made my day."

A desk clerk waltzed in with two large pizzas and set them down. "Mind if I help myself to a tip?"

"Please do."

She grabbed a slice and hurried out. Schak leaned over the table to snag his share. "Nobody tell my wife."

They all smiled. Schak's diets rarely made it to the end of the week.

"I thought Carl was a drug runner." Lammers reached for a slice. "How do we know Sam shot him?"

Jackson was ready for that. "The shotgun in his truck matches the bullet wounds, and the techs are processing his house now. I'm sure they'll find his brother's blood."

Lammers shuddered. "Kidnapping, rape, and murder. He's a real piece of work."

"Sex trade trafficking too," Dallas cut in. "He tried to sell the woman to me in an online forum."

"A psychopath." Evans turned to Dallas. "How did the feds get onto Sam?"

"Analysts found a pattern of sexual assaults in Vancouver, Washington." The agent reached for some pizza. "They sent me up there as bait. When we busted the rapist in the act, he gave us the online profile name *JungleBoy*. He'd posted in the incel forums about kidnapping a woman for sex."

"And you found him using the Strava app?" Evans shook her head.

"Pretty late in the game." Dallas' tone was self-deprecating.

"No, just in time," Jackson countered. "Sam might have made it out of the country if you hadn't shown up. I had no idea he'd kidnapped anyone."

"Are we sure he was running?" Evans asked.

"His passport was in the truck, along with a stack of cash." Jackson finally helped himself to a slice. "We can only guess where he was headed, but my money is on Costa Rica, where Sam and Carl grew up."

Dallas nodded. "The bureau sent me what background they could find. Apparently, their mother fled to Central America after dealing with children's services here in Eugene. She raised the kids in a weird fruitarian cult, then died of Crohn's disease a few years ago."

"What the hell is a fruitarian?" Schak sputtered, cheese sticking to his chin.

"I don't want to know." Jackson hoped to wrap-up quickly. He had other tasks and wanted to take the afternoon off. "Anything else?

"No real update on the Target kidnapping," Lammers said. "But it seems obvious that it's not connected to these cases, and the patrol sergeant thinks it's gang related." She drummed her fingers, looking like she wanted to leave, then asked, "How's Bettina Rios doing?"

"I called the hospital this morning. She and the baby are both fine." Jackson knew Bettina would never be the same. That kind of trauma permeated a victim's DNA and affected every aspect of their life. She would be grieving soon too. "Her mother died from neglect—another victim."

"Aaron Russo as well," Evans added. "He killed himself because he thought the woman he loved was dead."

For a long moment, they were all quiet.

Jackson sighed. So much damage from one selfish man who'd thought sex was more important than anything else. Jackson's faith in humanity deteriorated a little every day. "If we're done here, I'm heading out to North McKenzie to see Bettina."

"I'll go with you," Dallas said. "My flight isn't until tomorrow and I'm sick of hotel rooms."

Chapter 52

Jackson stood next to the hospital bed, realizing how petite and pretty Bettina was. He'd barely seen her on that dark little island before she was loaded into the helicopter. Bettina opened her eyes and glanced around, looking scared.

The nurse, who'd brought them in, said gently, "This is Detective Jackson and Agent Dallas. Do you feel like talking to them? You don't have to."

Bettina blinked a few times, then whispered, "Are you here to deport me?"

The poor woman. "No. Not at all." Jackson spoke softly, wondering if he should just leave. He wanted to be helpful, but he had more bad news. "I'll find you an immigration lawyer and other resources if you need them. I just wanted to see you and make sure you're okay." His phone buzzed in his pocket, but he ignored it.

Bettina nodded and looked back and forth between Dallas and him. "You were both there. You saved me."

Dallas stepped forward. "You saved yourself. Well done."

"You have great aim." Jackson smiled. "And you know how to fire a weapon."

"My father taught me . . . before a *buchon* killed him." Tears filled her eyes. "Is Mama dead? I keep asking but no one will tell me."

Jackson reached for her hand. "I'm so sorry. She had a heart attack, so she passed quickly and didn't suffer." There was no reason to tell her the ugly truth.

"I knew she was gone." Bettina wept, sobbing quietly. When she'd calmed, she said, "I'll have to give up this baby too, and then I'll have no one."

Her grief overwhelmed him. Jackson stepped away, blinking back his own tears. If Bettina hadn't been a surrogate, her disappearance might have gone unnoticed. He wondered how many other non-documented women suffered crimes the police never knew about. He would let Bettina learn about her ex-boyfriend's suicide from someone else, hopefully not anytime soon.

Dallas rescued them both by saying, "Hey, I brought you some pizza. I know how skimpy the meals are here."

Bettina laughed and cried at the same time. "Gracias. I love pizza."

While she ate a slice, a doctor came in to check his patient. Jackson and Dallas excused themselves. His phone buzzed again, but he was afraid to check it. He wasn't ready for a new case—or any pressure from Lammers to hold a press conference.

Outside the room, Dallas shook her head. "I hope she gets some counseling. That's too much for one person to deal with."

"No kidding." He thought he might make a mental health appointment for himself. They started down the hall. "What's next for you?" he asked.

"A short break in Flagstaff with my boyfriend, then I'll probably get back to work on this incel investigation. There are dozens more men to locate and check out." Dallas stopped, her pain obvious. "Most are probably just blowhards talking shit about things they'll never have the courage to do. But as we've learned, a few act out their aggressions and fantasies."

"You should probably let your leg heal."

Dallas smiled. "I can do that sitting at a desk." She started toward the elevator. "I promised myself I'd never look at the No Consent forum again, but I need to help find a freak who calls himself *KingCock*. I'm pretty sure he kidnapped someone."

Jackson's phone buzzed again. He tensed, then glanced at it. *Sophie.* He turned to Dallas, excused himself, and grudgingly took the call. "What now?"

"Jackson! Finally! This is important."

"I hope so."

Her words tumbled out. "A weird thing happened at work on Saturday, and it's been bugging me. This morning, after you said Sam had kidnapped Bettina, I couldn't stop thinking about what I saw and all the connections."

"What's this about?" He tried to suppress his impatience. Probably some research the reporter had done and wanted to share. Jackson glanced over and saw Agent Dallas signaling him to put the phone on speaker. As he did, they stepped into a small visitor room for privacy.

Sophie took a breath before launching in again. "I went into my boss' office to have him sign my timesheet and he was talking with someone, using his desk phone. He had his back to me, looking out the window." She paused for a moment.

"And?" Jackson had no idea where she was going, but he was mildly intrigued.

"While I waited, I glanced at his cell phone. He had just come in from a smoke break outside, and it was on his chair and open to a weird webpage." She cleared her throat. "So I picked it up for a closer look. Yes, that's snooping, but I'm a reporter so it's allowed. Anyway, the site was called No Consent."

A tingle ran up Jackson's spine.

Sophie talked faster now, her voice quiet. "It's a forum where men post deviant sexual fantasies about date rape and hurting prostitutes"—she paused for effect—"and abducting women as sex slaves."

Good god. He knew the forums existed, but he'd never had a reason to focus on the content.

Dallas abruptly grabbed the phone, her voice urgent. "Tell me what you saw. I need persona names, in particular."

"I think he was posting as *KingCock.*"

Dallas sucked in a breath. "What's your boss' name?"

"Hoogstad."

The agent started for the elevator. "Let's go get him."

Chapter 53

Thursday, September 26

Jackson sat in the lobby of the counseling center, wondering if he could really do this. He hated talking to people about his personal life. Maybe it would be easier with a stranger. To get comfortable, he would start with his job. The kidnappings disturbed him so deeply, he dreamed about them. Especially the last one . . . which had actually happened first.

When they'd raided Hoogstad's home, they'd found a woman in a locked room who'd been there for eight years. The sight of her—gaunt, bruised, and dead-eyed—had sickened him. He couldn't stop thinking about how many more like her were out there. Over the years, he'd seen news stories about long-term captivities, but those were easy to not think about. Other cities, different police departments, not his immediate concern. But now, it had happened in his hometown. Where his daughter lived. His friends' daughters and sisters too. How could he keep them all safe? How could he sleep at night, knowing women were being held as prisoners, praying for someone to rescue them?

The receptionist called his name, and Jackson followed her to a small office. Inside, an older woman stood and greeted him. After introductions, they both sat down. She smiled warmly and asked, "What are your primary concerns that bring you here today?"

Jackson swallowed hard, feeling like he might burst into tears. "I think I've made a mistake."

"What kind of mistake?" Her non-judgmental tone gave him the courage to say it.

"I moved in with my girlfriend and her grandson, but I don't think it's making me happy." He paused, but the counselor sat quietly. He tried to articulate his feelings. "I worry that the longer I stay with her, the harder it will be to leave. Not just for me, but for all of us."

"Do you love her?"

"Yes, she's a wonderful person."

"So what's the problem?"

Time to admit the truth. "I love another woman more."

L.J. Sellers writes the bestselling Detective Jackson mysteries—a five-time Readers Favorite Award winner. She also pens the high-octane Agent Dallas series, the new Extractor series, and provocative standalone thrillers. Her 26 novels have been highly praised by reviewers, and she's one of the highest-rated crime fiction authors on Amazon.

Detective Jackson Mysteries:
 The Sex Club
 Secrets to Die For
 Thrilled to Death
 Passions of the Dead
 Dying for Justice
 Liars, Cheaters & Thieves
 Rules of Crime
 Crimes of Memory
 Deadly Bonds
 Wrongful Death
 Death Deserved
 A Bitter Dying
 A Liar's Death
 A Crime of Hate
 The Black Pill

Agent Dallas Thrillers:
 The Trigger
 The Target
 The Trap

Extractor Series:
 Guilt Game
 Broken Boys
 The Other

Standalone Thrillers:
    The Gender Experiment
    Point of Control
    The Baby Thief
    The Gauntlet Assassin
    The Lethal Effect

L.J. resides in Eugene, Oregon where many of her 26 novels are set and is an award-winning journalist who earned the Grand Neal. When not plotting murders, she enjoys standup comedy, cycling, and zip-lining. She's also been known to jump out of airplanes..

Thanks for reading my novel. If you enjoyed it, please leave a review or rating online. Find out more about my work at ljsellers.com, where you can sign up to hear about new releases. —L.J.

Made in the USA
Coppell, TX
28 September 2021